HUNTRESS

Karina Kantas

Copyright © 2010 Karina Kantas

Paperback 3rd edition © Karina Kantas 2022

Dirty Streets Press Imprint

ISBN: 978-1-912996-52-0

Ride to live, live to ride!

Review Quotes

A very awesome book cover, great font & writing style. Wow, a very well written gang thriller book. It was very easy for me to read/follow from start/finish & never a dull moment. There were no grammar/typo errors, nor any repetitive or out of line sequence sentences. Lots of exciting scenarios, with several twists/turns & a great set of unique characters to keep track of. This could also make another great gang thriller movie, or better yet a mini-TV series. A very easy rating of 5 stars.

Huntress was a surprising yet wonderful read. I applaud Karina Kantas in tackling many intense and controversial topics with complete ease AND still writing an epic romance that leaves you wanting more.

This story was full of twists and turns as well as suspense. I really enjoyed this story. It had action, adventure, romance, and violence. Everything you would expect from a good MC story. I recommend this story to anyone looking for a good MC book.

It is fast paced [or maybe I just read it really fast because I loved it!] and the characters are developed with a healthy dollop of human nature.
If you are looking for a thrilling read, that includes the world of sordid affairs, sexy love and superb creativity – then I would STRONGLY suggest you pick this one up.

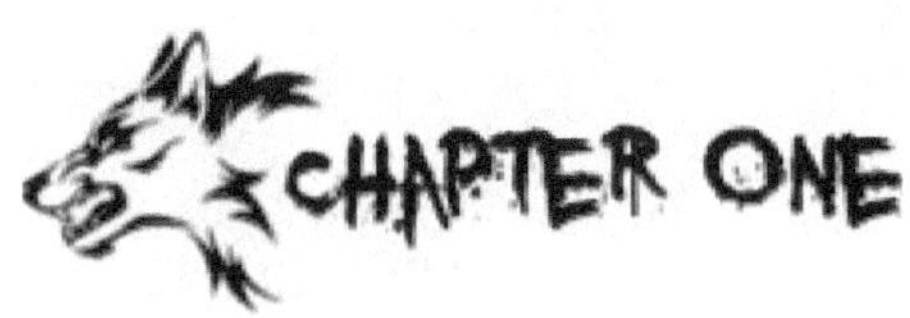

CHAPTER ONE

Okay, I might not be the smartest woman in the world, but that doesn't mean I'm dumb enough not to have realised that all was not what it seemed when it came to my parents.

Although they attempted to hide their true nature behind airs and graces, Jade, my mother, let her tongue slip occasionally. And when my parents argued, boy could they swear. It was like an explosion, as though they'd been holding it in for too long. All of a sudden, they would remember themselves, look at one another in disgust and then return to their charade.

Another clue that the pretty picture was a painting after all, was their association with Beth and Clay, two hard-core bikers; bikers that didn't have a problem popping pills or smoking marijuana in front of me. In fact, when they deemed me old enough, they offered me my share.

My brother John took an overdose and killed himself when he discovered the truth. He was only twenty-two.

I suppose I blame myself, but John should never have read my diary.

Clay is my godfather. My father, Marcus, was the best man at Beth and Clay's wedding. He's always been straight with me; told me how it was whether I could take the truth or not.

One late, warm afternoon, the three of us were sitting on their veranda chatting, when I dared to bring up the taboo subject of my parents' first meeting.

What Beth and Clay revealed changed my outlook on life. It changed who I was.

***

"So, why have you never brought this up before, Sofi?" Beth asked.

"I've wanted to talk to you about this many times; I'm guessing being stoned might have given me the courage."

"You know you only had to ask," she said.

"Yeah, I don't have a problem discussing it," Clay added. "Although I know Jade and Marcus would rather forget it."

Beth left her seat and entered the house. Clay passed me another beer; it was cold and soothing. My throat felt raw from smoking too many joints. My skin was clammy and my long brown hair was beginning to stick to my face and neck, so I tied it in a ponytail and then pulled my Iron Maiden t-shirt out of my jeans and tied it in a knot. I didn't realise it was going to be so warm. I would have been a lot more comfortable in my cotton pyjamas.

Clay looked like a typical beer-drinking biker. A large, muscular man, with medium length, white bushy beard, and he always wore soiled jeans and an old tatty T-shirt. But if you could see past his appearance, you'd find one of the nicest blokes you could wish to meet.

I'd yet to see his temper, but I could imagine if matched with someone his size, Clay would come out on top.

Beth returned and handed me a large photo.

A group of sixteen bikers stood in front of a line of impressive motorbikes. They all wore jeans or leathers, and looked tough.

The women were sexy; dressed in tight leather trousers and sleeveless black tops. I recognised Beth straight away; dark curly hair, small frame and huge smile. Apart from some grey hairs and wrinkles around the eyes, she hadn't changed much. Clay hadn't changed much either, he still had that knowing smile.

He pointed, and named each person in the photo.

"Was this your gang?" I asked.

"No. It was your dad's."

I choked and coughed out the smoke.

"That's your dad," Clay said, pointing to the biker standing in the middle of the group. His foot was resting on the front tyre of a bike. I guessed the red-head who was standing beside him was my mum.

"Jesus Christ!" I said, not believing what I was looking at.

The biker did look like a younger version of my father. Although his hollow cheeks had filled out, and I'd never seen him wearing anything other than shirts and trousers.

My mother gave me the biggest shock. She was wearing tight, black leather trousers, and a black T-shirt cut at midriff. Her eyes were lit up, her cheek rosy and she wore a contented smile. Her hair was waist length and bright red. Very different from the short, brunette hair I was accustomed to.

So many times I had caught her staring at my brother with a sorrowful expression and empty eyes.

I never understood until I saw that photo.

Clay allowed time for the revelation to sink in. Then passing me another joint, he told me all about the Tyrants.

"So, you were never a member?" I asked Beth, once they finished their account.

"No. I hung out with them, but Jade was the only female member. I think the guys preferred it that way. They treated her like a sister, you know, like one of the family."

"Weren't you jealous?" I asked.

"Nah. I wasn't after attention. I had my man. There was no jealousy between your mum and me. We've always been good friends."

"Did she always dress like this?" I asked, trying to picture the Jade I knew dressing similarly.

"That's nothing. You wouldn't believe half of the outfits she used to wear." Beth laughed.

"So she was a biker's tart?" I said, feeling disgrace.

"Jade had... has class. She used her looks and personality to draw men to her. But she wasn't free property. She belonged to Marcus and everyone knew that. She was tough. You should have seen her fight. It was something to watch."

"A hell cat," Clay added with a grin.

"And did you love her?" I asked him.

"We all did. It was hard not to fall in love with her charm. As Beth said, she was like a sister to us."

Clay then told me about my mother's rape and how the Tyrants went after the Vipers, their sworn enemies. My cigarette burned away in the ashtray, long forgotten, as I imagined what she must have gone through; the abduction, assault. In my mind, I saw four men holding her down while they injected her with drugs. I shuddered and pushed the image away.

My mind wouldn't allow it to sink in. This wasn't the Jade and Marcus I knew. There was no way these tough violent gang members were my parents. I needed more answers.

"We were the number one gang in London," Clay explained. "People feared us and we lived up to that reputation. Marcus was our fierce leader, Jade became his lady after fighting off the competition."

"Tell me about it," I urged.

"I can see this is going to be a long night," Beth said, standing up. "I'd better call your father and let him know you've arrived safely."

I allowed Beth and Clay to talk for hours about the Tyrants and the violent fights they had. It sounded exciting and dangerous, but I still couldn't visualise my parents in that situation.

They had hidden their past well; maybe even believing their own hype.

My heart started to race, my pulse quickened. Why had they kept this from me? Were they ashamed? Did they walk away from the gang because she was pregnant with me? How could they live a lie for so long? Did they want to rip off their disguise and be who they really were? Were John and I keeping them from living their life?

I took a long steady breath before lighting up yet another Joint

"Does John know any of this?" I asked

"I doubt it," Clay answered. "And I don't want him finding out right now. He's got enough distractions." Referring to John's ex-girlfriend's announcement that she was pregnant.

"Okay, I won't say anything," I shrugged.

Inhaling the smoke, I held it in and then let out a long breath. I was feeling pretty wasted and depressed.

"Now I know why Mum's not happy. They didn't want us. We were a mistake," I cried.

"You shut the hell up," Clay barked. "I don't want to hear you talking like that. They love you very much. You don't know the whole story."

"Then for Christ's sake tell me," I yelled. "I'm eighteen

now. I deserve to know the truth. If you don't tell me, I'll find out for myself."

"It's time she knew," Beth said.

"You're not going to like what you hear, Sofi," Clay warned.

"I'm ready."

Taking the discussion and drinks inside, we got comfortable in the living room and then Beth went to the kitchen for munchies. Man, I was hungry and yet my stomach felt weird. I wasn't sure if I could keep anything down. I think it was nerves. At last, I was going to learn what the big secret was.

"Who's this?" I asked, pointing to another biker standing next to my dad.

"That's Dylan," Beth said, "Marcus's older brother."

"My uncle," I whispered.

I could certainly see the family resemblance. But why had nobody mentioned him before?

The truth never occurred to me.

"He was killed in a knife fight." Clay told me.

I couldn't take my eyes off him as he told me the story.

"So he was defending the Tyrant's name?" I asked, after he had finished. "He was standing up for my dad."

Beth nodded. "He died in your mother's arms. Marcus didn't know anything about the fight, and he lost it when he saw Dylan's body."

"It hurt Jade the most," Clay added. "You see what Marcus didn't know, was Dylan and Jade were a lot closer than he thought, than any of us thought."

"They were sleeping together," I said, surprised.

"Yeah, but it wasn't as straightforward as it sounds," Beth answered.

"Your mum wanted the status as the head of the Tyrant's woman. Marcus wanted a beautiful woman by his side, at his disposal. Both were looking for trophies and both found what they were looking for. I'm not sure when it first happened between your mum and Dylan, but it was obvious something was going on."

"Didn't my dad care? He must have known if the rest of you figured it out."

Clay shook his head. "They never came out and announced they were in love; they kept their relationship secret. Dylan was too afraid of hurting his brother and I think Jade couldn't face the truth."

"She was too chicken-shit," I spat.

"Hey, she wasn't the only one playing the field," Beth injected.

"Yeah, your father was far from being a saint. His rendezvous with other women made it easier for your mum and Dylan to continue their affair."

"And they lived happily ever after," I added sarcastically.

"Not at all. They were planning to leave the Tyrants. They were going to tell Marcus. They started to make plans and then Dylan was murdered, by a Wolf called Mud."

"That's why your mum and dad left town," Beth continued. "She testified that a member of the Wolves killed Dylan. No one snitches on another gang member, whether they wear different colours or not. It's one of the rules."

"Yeah, but the Wolves didn't play by the rules did they." Clay slammed his fist on the table, the whisky glasses rattled.

"Your mum got a death threat as she was leaving the courthouse. Marcus knew he had to get the three of them out of town. The Tyrants officially disbanded that night."

It took a while before I realised what he'd said.

"Three of them? She was pregnant with John, wasn't she?"

Clay nodded.

I didn't want to ask, because looking down at the photograph I already knew the answer.

"Dylan was John's father, wasn't he?"

"Yes. There is no doubt he was," Clay answered.

"And you knew all this time? Why didn't you tell me?" I yelled.

"When Jade told me she was pregnant, I figured out the rest. She made me promise not to say anything to Marcus. I gave my word."

"How could he not know?" I stood up and paced the room. "Why haven't they told me? Fuck! My life is one big lie. I didn't know I had an uncle until tonight, now I find out he's my brother's father, and he's dead. This is turning out to be some fucking night."

"I did warn you." Clay shrugged.

"Anything else you'd like to tell me? Anything you've left out? What about me. Is Marcus my father?"

Beth nodded. "Yes, and he's still John's dad. He's the one that brought you both up."

"He's John's uncle, not his fucking dad," I screamed, flinging my arm across the mantle piece. Their wedding photo flew through the air. Shards of glass splintered as it crashed on the floor.

"Give the woman something to calm her down," Clay said.

Beth jumped off the couch and ran into the kitchen. She came back and handed me a red pill.. Taking a large gulp of warm, flat beer, I swallowed the pill and then slumped back down on the sofa. I was willing to take anything that would numb my pain. I trusted Beth and Clay not to give me something that would hurt me.

It took ten minutes before the drug started to take effect. I felt relaxed and blissful. My anxiety disappeared and it didn't occur to me, I should be feeling miserable after what I'd just been told.

The drug kept me awake until the early hours of the morning. As the effects started to wear off, my thoughts returned and reality came crashing back.

My father was a property developer. He spent his time sitting behind a desk, dressed in a shirt and tie. I never once saw him get his hands dirty. To think of him greased up, tinkering with a motorbike was absurd. Yet he used to be a bad-arse biker and president of a violent gang. It was as though another world existed aside from the one I lived in, and the more I turned the pages of the book the more I wanted to experience this world.

And Mum, the apron-wearing housewife; once a biker's tart, caught in a love triangle. Tragedy strikes and the lover is killed. Jeez, if I didn't know Clay better, I would have said he made the whole thing up. But proof was sitting on the table beside my makeshift bed, and the camera never lies. This wasn't a one-shot deal, a Halloween fancy dress photo. Their lifestyle, the closeness of the brotherhood was evident in the way they stood, dressed, and the expression in each of the bikers' faces. They were proud of who they were and happy to live the life they did.

I tried to imagine what life as a member of the Tyrants was like. I wondered what had happened to the other members. Had they tried to cling to the image and lifestyle, like Beth and Clay? Or had they all turned into family men like my dad?

***

I'm a writer for a local newspaper. Writing helps me understand the world and myself better. When my thoughts are all messed up in my head, I can get them to make sense when I put them on paper. When Clay and Beth told me the truth that night, I needed closure. I wrote everything I'd learnt in my diary.

***

They never once blatantly blamed me for John's death. But I think Dad felt guilty knowing he should have told him the truth. It makes me wonder whether things would have turned out better if he had. Maybe John would still be alive.

Dad went berserk when he found out I was taking drugs; nothing hard-core, just the odd pill and marijuana joints. It wasn't a subject that came up at the dinner table.

I think Mum was torn between wanting to shelter me from the lifestyle she had run away from, and blaming me for taking away John, the last link to Dylan, although she never came out and said it.

When they found out who told me the truth about their past, they cut all ties with Beth and Clay. It didn't matter how much I argued in their defence. Jeez, I was smoking dope way before Clay offered me a joint.

Things were falling apart and I couldn't bear to watch two people I loved tear one another to pieces. The grief and shame was too much for my mother and for a while she lost the plot. I remember the state of the kitchen when she finished wrecking it. Her best dinner service, shattered in pieces on the floor. She even managed to pull the bloody cupboards off their hinges; God knows where she got the strength from. Dad took her straight to the doctor's and they put her on anti depressants which seemed to calm her.

I tried to let slide my father's comments about the way I dressed and my choice of music. I thought he was jealous. He saw a shadow of his former self emerging from his daughter, and I guess it brought back happy memories, as well as tragic ones. I bet he was itching to jump on a motorbike and take off into the sunset.

Instead, he carried on his charade as a respected family man. Didn't he realise the family he had was breaking apart? Didn't he care?

I'd had enough. I packed my suitcase and moved down to London to live with Clay and Beth until I could sort something out.

I was determined to learn all I could about the Wolves, about a biker's lifestyle. Beth and Clay never clued into the motives behind my questioning. What better way to get all the dirt than from two actual bikers? The Wolves had taken my uncle and my brother away from me. They'd fucked up my family. I wanted revenge.

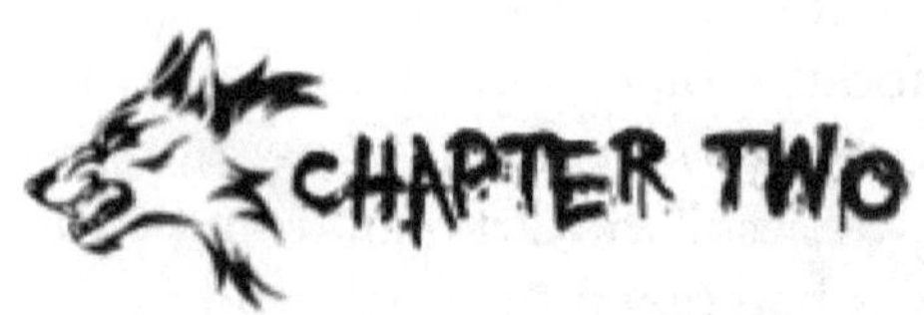

CHAPTER TWO

I was sitting at the breakfast table with Clay, sipping my morning coffee when I decided to bring up the subject of the Wolves again.

"Why did you stay in London, why didn't you leave town like the rest of the Tyrants?"

"Clay was adamant the Wolves weren't going to drive him from his home," Beth said, as she washed the plates. "When they found out the Tyrants had disbanded and Jade had left town, the Wolves vowed if she or Marcus ever came back to London, they'd be killed."

"Shit, they didn't do anything! The Wolves are the ones that murdered my uncle," I argued.

"You don't know how it was. There were rules. You never testify against another club member, no matter what patch he or she wears. We take care of our own."

"Then why didn't you?" I yelled, and then took a deep breath to calm myself. "Why didn't Dad get revenge and go after the Wolves?"

Clay shook his head. "The Tyrants were finished long before the Wolves came onto the scene. We were out of shape, out of practice, and no match for them. The Wolves stayed in the background watching us. They didn't pounce until they were ready, and by then they knew they would win."

"Win?" I asked.

Clay drank the last of his coffee as he stared at me.

"If the Wolves were to have any status in London, they had to get rid of the competition, the Tyrants. They weren't going to give us the opportunity of disbanding and walking quietly away. They wanted to finish it, and do it publicly, which of course they did."

"They got what they wanted," Beth said, "They were number one. The Tyrants were out of the picture. But when your mother testified in court and put a member of their gang behind bars. She became their number one enemy. As far as I know that hasn't changed."

Clay stood up and took his coffee mug over to the sink. "Come on, you're going to be late for work," he said.

I gulped down my warm coffee, bit into a slice of toast, and then gave my cup and plate to Beth.

"So the word is still out?" I asked, as I put my leather jacket on. "Do you really think that after twenty years, there are any original members left in the gang?"

"Maybe not," he answered. "That doesn't mean the death threat hasn't been carried down. Last I heard, there're about forty members in the East chapter, the one Mud Anderson runs, and they've got a good drug racket going."

I walked to the door with him and then we both reached up to the top shelf above the coat stand and took down our helmets.

"Have they given you any trouble?" I asked.

Clay opened the front door, and we walked out to the garage.

"They know who I am. They jeer, spit, and threaten, but it's all talk. They haven't laid a finger on Beth or me."

I nodded, and then put my helmet on before climbing onto my second-hand V Rod Harley. It wasn't a bad machine, just needed a good paint job, which Clay promised he'd do for me.

"Remind Beth I won't be home till late. I've got that audition with the band tonight."

"Oh, yeah. Good luck," he shouted back.

The roar of our motorbikes drowned out my reply.

We took off down the drive and then separated as we rode to our jobs.

***

I didn't want to meet the Wolves the same way Mum met the Tyrants. I wanted it to be a natural introduction, not look as though I was trying too hard. But I decided to follow her example and go straight for an officer of the pack. Surely, an officer's woman would receive more respect than the other females in the club. I just hoped the guys were attractive and not too old.

I guessed the easiest way to announce myself was to run in the same circles; hang out in biker bars, and hopefully be noticed.

I've always had a talent for singing so I came up with a delicious way of combining the two. I would join a rock band.

Although rock music was never played openly in my parents' house, I've always had the love for it. Singing in a band would get me into known biker bars, earn me respect from the punters, and hopefully I'd run into a Wolf or two. I hadn't decided where I was going to go from there. I knew it would take a while before I'd make a name for myself and maybe get some followers.

While riding to *London Weekly*, the newspaper where I worked, I sang the lyrics of "Love Walked In," one of my favourite rock tracks by Thunder. It was going to be my audition song.

A pair of blue jeans and a tight black T-shirt were folded in my satchel, ready to change into after work.

I'd only been working at the paper for a month when the editor started giving me my own assignments. I loved the challenge of a deadline and my articles never failed to impress. That morning, I was interviewing a woman who had sold her baby over the internet. I knew the article would cause a stir.

As the day progressed, I became more anxious about the impending audition. What if they're weren't impressed? Could I take rejection? I had my heart set on getting this gig, I never thought of the negative side. What if the band was crap and couldn't play? How would I turn them down?

I needn't have worried. When I walked into the church hall, the band was already rocking hard. The three guys in their late twenties certainly looked the part of rockers; long hair, ripped jeans and black T-shirts advertising heavy metal bands. These guys knew how to play too. The moment they saw me, they stopped playing and one of them shouted out "hi."

"You guys rock," I said.

My anxiety disappeared as the lead guitarist played a riff in response to my comment.

I introduced myself, and the drummer immediately offered me a can of beer. I turned down the offer. It didn't matter to me that they liked their drink; I wanted to make a good impression and didn't want to be known as a drinker. Plus, I preferred whisky.

The church hall, with no furniture and bare walls, had perfect acoustics. I was itching to sing.

Standing by the mike with an amp monitor in front of me, I belted out "Love Walked In." They sat up in their seats and leaned in to whisper to one another. I knew they were impressed. When I finished, Todd, the lead guitarist, asked me if I knew the lyrics to "Sweet Child of Mine."

"Who doesn't," I answered.

It felt as though we'd been playing for months. Everything fell together. The rhythm and timing were spot on. Greg, the bass guitarist, sang with me and his vocals harmonized perfectly with mine.

We were so excited about the electric performance, we went through another four songs before taking a break. Of course I didn't know all the lyrics, so I made up most of the words. The guys laughed at my crude sense of humour.

Before I left the hall late that evening, Todd gave me a tape of the songs I had to learn. Our first gig was a week on Saturday and the next practice session in two days. I assured them I would know the lyrics by then.

We practiced every night, came up with ChainMail as the band name, and Jake, the drummer, suggested Dior as my stage name.

***

I wasn't sure whether to invite Clay and Beth to my first gig. However once they knew where we were playing there was no stopping them.

To say I had the jitters before I went on was an understatement. I heard the quiver in my voice when I first started singing and expected the audience to pelt me with rotten fruit. Once I sighted Beth and Clay, I kept my eyes on them until I began to relax and enjoy the experience. Although it was a pub known for its live rock music, there weren't many bikers in the audience. In fact, there wasn't much of an audience. The ones that were listening thankfully stayed for the whole set. They didn't call for an encore, and I was grateful. The adrenalin that had kept me pumped through the performance now left both my body and my vocal cords exhausted.

After I packed away my equipment, the guys joined me at Clay and Beth's table. Introductions were made and then Clay gave us his opinion.

"You should loosen up more," he told me. "You're too stiff. You're not singing slow love songs, you know?"

Clay had been drinking.

"Give her a chance," Beth said. "It was her first live performance, there were bound to be nerves."

I smiled at her.

"Well, we think you did a terrific job," Todd said. "The crowd loved you. Landlord's already signed us up for another gig next week."

"That's terrific," I said, and then yawned. "But Clay's right. I do need to loosen up on stage. I remember watching other singers and thinking the same thing. The audience isn't just here to hear us; they're scrutinizing us as well. We need to give them something to watch."

"You know what you need," Clay slurred. "You need some sort of act; something that will liven up the performance."

For days, I thought about what he said. Yes, we needed an act, something that would get audience participation. A reaction from them rather than having them staring at me with dead eyes, which was so off putting and wasn't helping my confidence.

It took a month to perfect my performance.

I started the show dressed in tight, leather trousers and a black, baggy jumper. I left my long curly hair loose, and my silver gothic make-up sparkled under the stage lights. The first song I sang was a slow but rocky Bon

Jovi number. Standing behind the microphone, I swayed to the beat but wouldn't leave my spot. By the time the first half of the set had finished, the bar room was full. I ran out backstage, re-touched my makeup, adjusted my outfit, and took a quick drink, shared a joint with the guys, and then it was back on stage. One more slow song and it was time to liven things up.

"So you ready to rock!" I shouted.

The audience whistled and cheered. Then I took off my jumper and revealed a black, front laced, plastic corset, which left little to the imagination. The place erupted in cheers. Next, I belted out a fast rocky number called "Heart 16."

I didn't just get male attention; the females swayed and clapped as well. I moved around the stage as if I owned it and that just got the crowd going wilder.

Three months passed, and the act was already getting old. We had quite a following, and I would see the same faces at gigs. The problem was they knew what was coming. I'd have guys shouting "get 'em out," even before I'd get to the end of the first set. Still, I think everyone had a good time no matter how many times they'd heard us performing the same songs.

The night I'd been waiting for finally arrived. I met the president of the Wolves. But it wasn't how I imagined it would be.

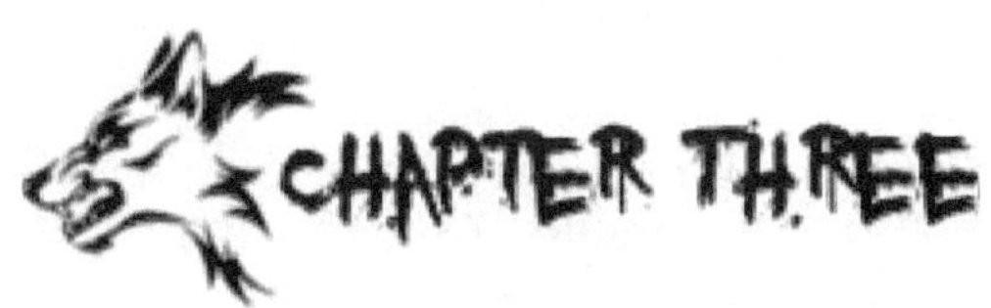

CHAPTER THREE

We were playing a gig in the Two Thorns, a classic bikers' pub. Dingy, with worn furniture and tough-looking bar staff; one girl had around a dozen piercings in her face and purple hair—not a great look.

We'd never played there before and the crowd proved hard to please. Half of the male audience looked as though they didn't want to be there. I even saw someone yawn. I knew I couldn't keep them waiting. The music had to get heavy. I'd just finished a Pat Benatar number, when I turned to the band and told them to turn up the heat. They nodded and started the intro to "Heart 16." I took off my jumper and the male bikers in the bar drowned out my voice with whistles.

I felt lethargic, as though I was coming down with something, but I knew I had to give them a great show. I doubted they would stand for anything less. I gave my all, putting every bit of energy into my performance.

At half time, I sat in the dressing room with my eyes closed. It wasn't really a dressing room, more like a large cupboard, but it had hooks, chairs and a closing door, enough to have a little privacy. It was sweltering inside the pub and the small fan I had in the dressing room blew nothing but warm air back on me. My head was throbbing and I felt feverish, but the show had to go on. Todd was concerned and told me I looked faint. I smiled at him weakly and then took the pill Greg offered. I was too tired to recognize if it was an upper or a downer.

I hoped the drug would keep me going until the end of the set, and that I wouldn't start freaking out on stage.

Jake wasn't fond of popping pills and had a go at Greg for giving me the drug. An argument kicked off, leaving me with a worse headache.

The night when I needed to be on my toes and give my best performance was turning out to be the worst gig yet.

To top it all, through the second set, a member of the audience was annoying me. I recognized him from previous shows, but that night he was wasted. I tried to ignore the obscene remarks, he was throwing my way, but his volume kept getting louder. A couple of bikers who were enjoying the show made their annoyance known. I thought a fight was going to break out. However, no one threw any punches.

I was finishing off the set like I normally did, with a song called "Look But Don't Touch". The words were supposed to be taken literally. I had a flirty dance sequence that went with the performance, and although I didn't feel up to it, I still performed. For some reason, the drunk seemed to think my routine was just for him. He stood licking his lips and rubbing himself and then made the mistake of trying to get onto the stage. He grabbed at my ankle, but I wasn't having any of it. I kicked him away, adding some verbal remarks as well. The bikers had had enough and showed him the door.

There was no encore this time. I was relieved to get

off the stage. Back in the dressing room, I collapsed onto the chair. Todd told me to go home, and they would pack up the gear. Jake wanted to phone for a taxi, but there was no way I was leaving my Harley in the pub car park all night.

A few customers remained by the bar finishing off their pints. The rest of the audience had left. I said goodnight to the bar staff and then walked out into the cool night air, hoping it would refresh me, but it just made me feel worse. I felt light-headed and wasn't sure if I could ride my bike home. I was thinking seriously of taking up Jake's offer of a taxi.

A couple of cars and a few motorbikes were still out front. I walked around the back to where Todd's Transit van and my Harley were parked. I had my helmet in the fold of my arm and the key to my bike in my right hand. I was only a few steps from my bike when someone grabbed me from behind.

One hand covered my mouth; the other hand grabbed my arm. My helmet fell to the tarmac. Pinning my arm behind my back, the guy dragged me away from my bike and toward a dimly lit lane next to the pub. I kicked, screamed, and bit into his hand, petrified, refusing to think about what he wanted to do with me. He slapped me hard around the mouth and threw me to the ground. I tasted blood again but knew it was my own. My mouth throbbed and I felt sick.

A low-toned voice growled, "I've been waiting for you, you fucking whore! You've been teasing me all night, now you're going to get it."

I yelled out for help and cursed, but that seemed to excite him more. All I got was a glimpse of a brown jacket and unshaven face before he brought his fist up and thumped me in the stomach. It felt as though a car had ploughed into me. I couldn't breathe. Winded and stunned, the guy took the opportunity and started to undo the zip of my jeans.

"Hey!" Someone yelled.

The drunk jumped to his feet and took off down the lane. Two guys ran after him while another one knelt down beside me.

"You okay?" he asked.

I nodded but didn't dare to speak. I was shaking and didn't want to show my fear in front of him. I recognized him as a customer from the pub. Yes, I'd been checking him out. The guy would have caught my eye in a stadium of bikers. He had medium-length, wavy hair, smooth, dark looking skin, and chocolate coloured eyes.

Even wearing my leathers, the coldness of shock was biting at my skin. I shivered. He started to take his jacket off.

"You're not supposed to give away your colours," I said.

Laying the jacket around my shoulders, I felt his body warmth and breathed in the scent of his aftershave; woodland trees and spice; very musky and very male.

"You know the code?" He questioned.

"I've been around."

"Trent's got your hood," he said, referring to my helmet. "That's a mean machine you've got there. Who did the paint job?"

"A friend," I replied. "Thanks for your help, but please take your colours back before you get into trouble."

"Rules are supposed to be broken," he answered with a smile.

The two bikers ran back up the lane.

"We lost him," one said, as he bent over breathlessly.

"Did you get a good look at him?" The guy beside me asked.

"Yeah, it was Leonard,"

"Take care of it," he said.

His friends took off back down the alley.

I recognize an order when given. The biker had status. I was intrigued.

Another two of his friends, one male and one female, stood at the top of the alley looking directly at me. I didn't like them staring, so holding onto my Samaritan's arm, I pulled myself up.

"You sure you're okay?" He asked.

"I'm fine," I assured him.

But as I went to walk away, my legs trembled, and I fell into his arms. I was shaking, but refused to allow the tears to come.

Greg, Todd, and Jake arrived and came over to help.

We walked back inside the pub. The small group of bikers followed.

Sitting me down, Todd then stood over me while I drank a large brandy.

"Has anyone called the cops?" Jake asked.

"No need, it's taken care of."

Jake stepped forward as though to argue with the guy, but the lethal stare was enough to stop him from uttering another word.

Ten minutes later, everyone was still standing around me. I felt a lot calmer and didn't like the feeling of being crowded.

"You guys better go home. I'm fine," I said to the band.

"We'll give you a lift," Greg said.

"No problem. I'll make sure she gets home safely," my biker answered.

Jake's face said it all. There was no way he was leaving me alone with those guys. Did he know something I didn't?

"It's okay," I assured them. "I'll be fine. I'll call you when I get home."

They were still unsure about leaving.

My Samaritan nodded to one of his friends. At once, the front door of the pub was opened, informing the musicians it was time to leave.

"I'll be fine. Thanks," I called, as I watched them walk out.

Waiting until the door closed again, my biker then stood up and took one of his friends aside. He whispered something, but kept his sight on me. I smiled.

A moment later the woman was ushered out of the door. Knowing I had his attention, and that he was someone of position, gave me a thrill.

I wasn't afraid or nervous about being in the pub with the male bikers. The landlord, who had given me a small, plastic bag full of ice cubes, was behind the bar and keeping a watchful eye on things. He knew the bikers by name; I got a feeling they were regulars to the bar.

I looked at the guy who had rescued me, and smiled. "You don't have to stick around. You've done enough. I can get home okay." I winced, as my stomach cramped.

He smiled back and then handed me another drink. Man, that smile gave me the shivers. This guy was sex on legs.

I already guessed that the female who'd been shown the door was his woman, just from the way she stuck around and the deathly stares she'd given me.

Every spoken or silent order he gave, turned me on. I know I shouldn't have been feeling like that, especially with what had happened, but it was as though I had no control over my emotions. I couldn't help what I was feeling.

"So," I said, turning to face him. "I'm Dior, and you are?"

He smiled. "Name's Buzz Anderson, acting president of the Wolves. Pleasure to meet you, Dior." He held his hand out, but I didn't take it.

His name rang through my ears and bounced around in my head. My heart started racing.

"You're a Wolf," I whispered. "You're Mud's son?"

"Yeah, I guess you've heard of us then?" He stared hard at me.

"Like I said, I've been around." I turned my head away and began examining my scratched hand. I'd caught a glimpse of the patches on the guys' jackets but didn't think on it.

My shoulders felt heavy. The jacket was weighing me down. I stopped myself from shrugging it off.

Buzz noticed my suddenly cold attitude. He walked around to the front of my chair.

"You've got a problem with the Wolves," he cautioned. The change in the tone of his voice scared me. Suddenly I didn't want to be in the bar surrounded by a pack of wolves.

I stood up and allowed the jacket to fall to the floor. "I've got a fucking problem with all men, right now. Can't you understand that? Hell, I don't need this shit."

The bag broke when I slammed it down and ice cubes slid across the table and fell onto the floor. I pushed past him, grabbed my helmet from Trent, and then rushed out of the bar.

I stood outside beside my bike, breathed deeply, and cursed myself for being so stupid. I'd just walked away from the Vice President of the Wolves, who was now acting President, and who also happened to be gorgeous and charming. What the fuck was I thinking?

I rode back to Clay's, fast and hard. I was still raging when I arrived. Banging the door shut and throwing my helmet down on the floor, I stomped to the drink cabinet, poured Vodka into a glass and downed the drink. The liquid burned the back of my throat, but I liked the pain and so poured another.

Beth came down the stairs, dressed in a robe.

"What the hell's going on?" She asked.

"Shit—I'm sorry I woke you. I forgot you were sleeping."

"Yeah, well some of us got work in the morning. Not me of course. Hey, get me one of those then we can sit down, and you can tell me what a shitty night you've had."

She never mentioned my swollen bloody lip.

We sat curled up on the couch and talked for over an hour. I didn't tell her about what happened to me, or that I met the president of the Wolves.

I wanted to know what first attracted her to Clay. Why she stayed with him even knowing he was a Tyrant.

"It was his bad-boy image and the tattoos," she admitted. "But I soon realised there was another side to his hard exterior. He never tried to impress me with his toughness, but I saw what he was capable of doing. Don't get me wrong, he was like the rest of them. When they were together they were violent and tough, and Clay could be a mean son of a bitch, but just like the others, when they were out of the public eye, they were normal, friendly, caring guys. I quickly fell in love with him."

"Didn't you want in, though? Didn't you want to be a Tyrant?" I asked, as I emptied the last of the Vodka into my glass.

"No. It never appealed to me. Oh, I could hold my own if provoked, but I didn't want to live like that. I didn't want the respect or fear the Tyrants got. I had the best of both worlds. I was able to hang around with them, without being associated with the name."

"Yeah, but you had the opportunity. Didn't you wonder?" I argued.

"I saw enough to make up my mind. Think of how vicious and tough the Wolves are. Now, take away the drugs, and you have the Tyrants."

I suddenly wanted it all. I wanted the lifestyle, the brotherhood, the feared respect. I wanted to experience life as a member of a bikers' gang.

If I was going to go through with my plan, I needed answers, and I hoped Beth would have them.

"Tell me about the Wolves? I've seen them around town. They look tough. How did they start up?" I drained my glass and then rolled a joint.

"God, back in the Tyrant days, the Wolves were just a bunch of thugs. A far cry from what they are now."

"What changed?" I asked.

"Mud, the bastard who murdered Dylan. He changed things."

"How?"

Beth shifted in the chair. I could sense she didn't want to talk about it, but I needed to know. Before I saw Buzz again, I needed to know why.

Beth continued, "His real name is Simon Anderson—"

I took a deep drag, and passed her the joint.

"Yeah, but he's known as Mud. He was a member of the original Wolves; a pack of bikers who caused some trouble but nothing heavy. Tyrants were number one. The Wolves showed us respect until an argument kicked off in a pub and Dylan was murdered. I wasn't there, so I didn't see it happen. But it was Mud who stabbed your uncle." She held in the smoke for a few seconds and then blew it out. "He was sentenced to ten years but only served five. When he was released, that's when things changed. He hardened, turned vicious and dangerous, and the Wolves decided Mud was the leader they needed. I heard he's been in and out of jail ever since."

I was guessing Mud was back in jail, and that was why his son, Buzz, was acting president.

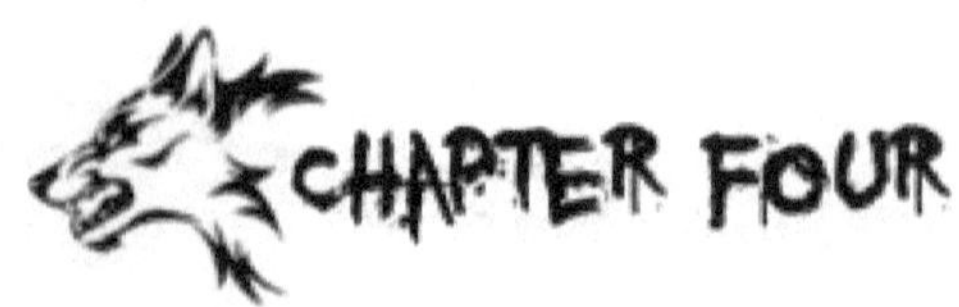

I met Buzz again at the weekend. I noticed him in the audience along with three other Wolves. He didn't take his eyes off me, and he was still hanging around after we'd finished the set.

"Hey, Dior. How's it going? I heard you were playing down here. Umm, can we talk?"

"Sure, let me just pack up my gear, and I'll meet you outside."

I ignored the looks Greg, Jake and Todd gave me. It only took me five minutes to get my gear back into the van.

I couldn't believe he'd made the effort to track me down. And I was nervous but excited at the thought of being around him again.

Buzz was outside leaning against his bike, a beautiful Dyna Low Rider, Harley. He was chatting to his friends when I walked up to them.

"Hey," I greeted.

"You wanna go for a ride?" Buzz asked.

Here was my chance to get closer to the Vice President. Even knowing he was a Wolf and what might happen if I was alone with him, it only took a second to decide.

"Yeah, sure. I'll leave my bike here, okay?" I answered with a smile.

The other Wolves got onto their bikes and took off. We went the opposite direction. Wrapping my arms around him, I held on tight. I couldn't wipe away the smile etched on my face. I was sitting on the back of a Wolf's ride. Oh, if Mum could see me now.

We took a tour around the bright lights of the city. London was still vibrant that late at night. I was caught up in the energy, the noise, the smells of the city, and was enjoying my ride so much, I felt a little disappointed when Buzz slowed and pulled over to the side of the road. I got off the bike and waited for him to park.

"Come with me," he said, and held out his hand.

I accepted his invitation and we walked across the road to the park. His hand was cold and smooth. I wanted to stroke his fingers.

The gate was closed and locked but that didn't stop Buzz. Climbing effortlessly up the sidewall, he swung his leg over the top and then reached down and pulled me up.

I sat on the wall and watched him jump down and then hold his arms out waiting to catch me.

We strolled hand in hand around the empty park. I wondered if we were going to talk at all, when he stopped walking.

"Dior, I'm sorry about the other night. I didn't mean to upset you. It was insensitive of me. It's just I get over protective when it comes to the Wolves' name. I overreacted. I hope you can forgive me."

"There's nothing to forgive." I said.

Man! I wanted to kiss him. The way he was looking at me made my legs turn to jelly. "I'm the one who should be apologizing. It was rude of me to leave like that, after all you'd done."

We continued walking. I wanted to ask him what he did to Leonard but decided not to bring it up.

"I was hoping I'd see you again," I said.

He turned, faced me, and then leaned in and kissed my lips. I pulled him to me and opened my mouth so the kiss could deepen. I wanted to feel and taste his tongue. His mouth was hot. My stomach quivered. I breathed in his scent and felt I was losing control. I wanted him to take it further. Nevertheless, whether he was playing hard to get or not, he slowed the kissing and then pulled away grinning.

We continued walking through the empty park, across grass that was damp from the evening mist. I put my arm around his waist while my hand held onto the pocket of his jeans. He laid his arm around my shoulder.

All thoughts of the Wolves left me. All that mattered then was how Buzz made me feel. It had been a long time, since I'd felt horny; and even longer since I'd had sex. If he didn't make the first move, I would.

"When you said you've been around, what did you mean?" he asked. "I've never seen you before that night."

His attention was fixed on me, and I wondered how much he could see.

"I'm a singer in a rock band. I've done gigs in most biker bars, so we move in the same circles. Everyone's heard of the Wolves."

"It doesn't bother you?"

I shrugged. "Why should it? I don't know you. Buzz is just a biker who I'd like to get to know better, intimately."

The word worked like magic. He pulled me to him and groped at my breasts as we kissed. I put my hands under his T-shirt and ran them up and down his toned chest. As his lips kissed and his tongue licked my neck, I sighed.

I wanted him. There would be no resisting.

"Dior," he whispered, as his hand undid the button and zip of my jeans.

I wanted him to feel what I was feeling.

He groaned, gasped, and increased his rubbing. A moment later I had an orgasm. For a few seconds, I lost all senses. He held me until my body stopped quivering and my panting calmed.

I wasn't going to leave him unsatisfied, so I knelt down on the grass in front of him.

Foreplay over, but no main event. We dressed in silence. I wondered why he didn't want to go all the way.

"You're something else," he said, as we walked back.

I was glad he felt that way, especially with how many women probably went down on him. I guess he wanted to take things slow. I got the feeling he wanted to see me again.

I could keep this guy satisfied, I told myself.

We climbed back over the wall and jogged across the road to the bike.

I felt comfortable sitting on the back of the bike with my arms wrapped around him. I wanted the feeling to last, and decided there and then that I was going to be seeing a lot more of Buzz.

"I'm glad we hooked up tonight," he said, as he sat on his bike in the pub car park.

"Yeah, me too. I'd like to get to know you better, Buzz. I like being around you."

"It's the colours and my title that makes women say that," he retorted.

"Fuck that." I answered. "I wanted you, even before I knew who you were."

He smiled, and my stomach quivered again.

"So, I'll see you around, Dior?"

"Hope so," I said, and then climbed on to my bike.

From my mirror, I saw him smiling, watching me ride away.

I'd had relationships before. I thought I'd been in love, but no man had caused me to react that way to a smile, a look. Buzz was the sexiest man I'd ever met.

I knew we'd meet up again.

Three days later, as I was riding into town, I recognized his bike in my mirror. I turned my head and he flashed his light. We pulled over and chatted for a few minutes, and then arranged to meet up after my gig that night. This happened four times. Each time we'd act like teenagers, walking together, groping, kissing, and fooling around, but we never had intercourse. No matter how much I wanted it, I never asked him why. I was just happy to have his time and company. He made me feel good about myself. He made me enjoy life again.

We'd been seeing each other on and off for about two weeks when he asked if ChainMail would consider doing a show at their clubhouse. I doubted the guys would agree after what happened at the pub that time. Buzz said he'd make it worth their while.

I assured Todd, Jake, and Greg it would be safe, and there wouldn't be any trouble. They reluctantly agreed. It would have been stupid to turn down the money Buzz was offering.

***

Trent and a Wolf named Hue were at the clubhouse when we arrived and were nice enough to give us a hand setting up the gear. A black curtain covered the back of our makeshift stage. The silver ChainMail banner looked fabulous on the black background.

The clubhouse was situated in the sticks, in the middle of nowhere. There was enough land to park a hundred motorbikes and no neighbours to complain about noise. This was theirs; a place where they could do what they wanted and fuck the rules. The clubhouse was more like a barn; a long wooden structure housing a wooden floored hall, bar, two pool tables and a jukebox. The only seating was six ripped, black plastic covered stools, which lined up against the bar. There were toilets and an office at the left of the hall, and a small room at the back, which we used as our dressing room. The clubhouse was nothing to rave about, but it was theirs, and I'm sure that's what made it damn special to them.

The Wolves started rolling up around eight PM. Greg and Jake stayed in the back while Todd and I had no problem mingling with the bikers. Once Todd started talking about his music, there was no stopping him. Buzz turned up around eight-thirty with his woman in tow. He came straight over and introduced himself to Todd, and then apologized for his behaviour the other week.

I knew Buzz wasn't really apologizing. He was playing a role; sweet-talking the entertainment so Todd would feel less nervous about playing for the Wolves. He asked how I was, the usual friendly banter. I noticed he didn't bother to introduce his woman.

Long, blonde, straight hair; she was tall, but thin and shapeless. Her face wasn't much to look at either. Maybe I was being unkind, because she had Buzz, and I didn't. But I did wonder what he saw in her. She stood silently by his side, as if she wasn't there. There was no way I would ever allow my man to diss me like that in public, even if he were the V.P of the Wolves.

"When do you want us to go on?" I asked Buzz.

I was still wearing jeans and T-shirt; I'd yet to change into the special outfit I'd bought for that night.

"Start the first set about nine-thirty. There'll be more coming in later."

The place looked crowded already; I could imagine how many Wolves would be there come eleven pm.

The bikers greeted one another with lengthy powerful hugs as though they were brothers that hadn't seen each other for years. There was so much love in the room; I was caught up in it. Gazing at Buzz in a seductive manner, I smiled.

His woman stepped forward and shoved me hard.

"Cut it out, Mandy," Buzz warned.

"Who the fuck does she think she is?" Mandy spat.

"She's a guest, and better be treated like one, or you can get the hell out of here," he retorted. "Now shut the fuck up."

Leaning in towards me, he whispered. "Meet me out the back in five."

I laughed sexily, as though he'd just said something funny.

A couple of bikers walked in and Mandy got Buzz's attention. They both walked away.

I left Todd chatting away and then went around the back to start getting ready. I was on such a high, without the use of any drugs. I couldn't wait to perform for them, but first I had to perform for Buzz.

Greg and Jake were still sitting in the back room. Both had bored expressions etched on their faces.

"What are you guys hiding in here for?" I laughed. "We'll be going on in twenty; you might as well go out there and get a beer. It's served cold," I smiled. "People want to meet you. They're not going to bite. Go and check it out. Todd's having a great time."

They took me on my word and left the room. I started to undress.

Buzz crept up behind me while I was doing up the laces of my boots.

"Meow," he said, eyeing up my costume of a black, tight, P.V.C cat suit, with a low front.

"You like?" I asked, and twirled.

"Come here pussy," he ordered.

Grabbing me, he pushed me up against the metal door and kissed me hard. We didn't have time to fool around. I knew what he wanted. Lifting up his sleeveless, black T-shirt, I kissed and nibbled his chest just giving him a taste of what was to come.

My teasing was driving him wild. He groaned and breathed heavily and then gently pushed my head down, while I continued kissing his body.

His groans of pleasure were enough to satisfy me.

When I'd finished servicing him, we embraced once more.

"Give em a good show, Dior," he said, and then left so I could touch up my hair and make up.

I didn't feel used. I didn't think of myself as a slut. It was a way for both of us to work away any tension. We enjoyed our intimate moments together. We needed each other. I don't know how Buzz felt, but I wanted more.

I performed for Buzz. I sang the songs to him. I danced for him. The Wolves got off on my performance and even more so when they realised I was flirting with their president. During my breaks, I made sure I was by his side as we pushed our way through the sea of leather, blue jeans, and testosterone.

He introduced me around and it didn't take long for the Wolves to figure I was more than a guest. I loved that I had his attention; I loved that the Wolves were attentive to me. Mandy glared at me throughout the night, I imagined she wanted to rip me apart; but while Buzz was around, there was nothing she could do, which caused me to flirt even more.

CHAPTER FIVE

Buzz never questioned where I was going when I told him I would be away for a couple of days. We were seeing each other nearly every night, and I needed a break. I had to get my shit together and start planning how I was going to get the Wolves to talk about Mud, the Wolf that killed Dylan, and whom I had yet to meet.

I wanted Buzz to promise me he wouldn't fuck around while I was gone, but I never mentioned it. I was the other woman, and for now I had to accept that.

I planned a surprise visit to Birmingham to see my parents. And boy was it a surprise. Mum came out the door, took one look at the bike and then walked back inside. Dad stood inside the doorway waiting. He was staring at me, but I knew he wasn't seeing me. I should have realised that turning up on a Harley, dressed in jeans and leathers would bring back memories for him.

He smiled as I approached.

"You are your father's daughter," he said.

After we hugged, I pulled away from him and looked into his face. "You're not mad?"

"I can't say I'm surprised. It doesn't matter how we brought you up, you have biker's blood in you. I'm glad you're here, Sofi. The three of us need to talk."

"I know. But do you think Mum will listen?"

"She'll come around; it was a shock seeing you like this. Hell, it was a blast of dèjà vu."

I took my jacket off, and I followed him into the house. Sitting down on the couch, I waited for Mum to acknowledge my presence.

Standing with her hands on her hips, she stared at me. "You want a drink, maybe a beer or a whisky? How about a joint?" she said with a sarcastic snarl.

"A coffee will do fine," I said.

I knew it was going to be hard, but I wasn't ready to justify myself.

Dad turned off the TV, and then we small-talked while waiting for Mum to return.

Instead of sitting down, she started to pace the room.

"Maybe if we'd talked about it, she would have never gone this route. If we'd been honest from the start, she wouldn't be living this lifestyle."

"Jesus Christ, Mum! I'm sitting right here. You can talk to me." I jabbed me finger into my chest. "I love bikers; I love rock music, I like the odd smoke, what's wrong with that? I'm not a fucking outlaw like the two of you were. I don't go around threatening and using violence to get respect."

Mum stared at me.

"I like who I've become, and no matter how much you wanted to shield me from this biker's lifestyle, this is who I am. Can't you understand that?"

"Yeah, but you only changed when you learnt about the Tyrants. Why is that?" she said.

I stood up and glared at them. "It has nothing to with the fucking Tyrants," I yelled. "It has nothing to do with

Clay or Beth, so you can both stop acting like children and mend this friendship, which I know is important to you. I was smoking and drinking way before your dark secret came out. Both of you should stop living this lie and start being yourselves again. You shouldn't deny who you truly are, so don't deny me my right. If you don't ever want to get on another motorbike again, that's fine. It's your choice. Being a biker, wearing leathers, doesn't make me an outlaw."

I said my piece, maybe more than I should, but I'd been waiting for a long time to give my speech and hopefully knock some sense into them.

"It's not as easy as you make it sound," Dad said. "You can't just switch the feeling on and off. Hell, the moment I saw you pulling up on your Harley, my fingers were itching to get on the throttle, but I know I'll probably never ride a bike again. It's just not who I am anymore."

"That's bullshit." I said.

"Well, I can see where she gets her mouth from," Dad replied.

I turned and looked at Mum. She was smiling. I wasn't sure if she should be, I feared she was losing it again.

"Mum. Mum, you okay?"

"I'm sorry." she said, and then laughed. "Just looking at you standing there dressed like that and listening to your language, reminds me of me twenty years ago."

"I was thinking the same thing," Dad said, then laughed.

Seeing both my parents laughing, started me off. It took a while before we all calmed.

"I'm not going to say I like this, and I'm not going to try to influence your decision. You're old enough to make your own choices, even if they are the wrong ones. You know, I was your age when I moved to London and met your father."

"Tell me about it," I urged.

Mum took my hand, as we sat down, and she told me about the first time she saw my father in the subway.

Their faces lit up as they told their stories of the fights and dangers they'd faced as Tyrants. The passion for the lifestyle was still there. They talked fervently about the other members' antics and violent incidents they'd experienced. Yes, I was seeing my parents in a different light. At last, they were coming out of their shells, and I understood where my love for fast bikes and hard rock came from.

I allowed them to talk until their throats became dry, then we hugged and cried. I think it was as much of a relief for them as it was for me to get everything out in the open. I was now the one living a lie.

Mum pulled me off the couch. "Come with me. I want to show you something."

I followed her upstairs and into their bedroom. Opening the closet, she then pulled down the loft door. I stood underneath as she climbed the ladder. I heard her moving things around, and then she lowered down a large, dust covered, oblong box. Taking the box, I placed it on the bed and blew off the top layer of dust. I waited until she joined me.

As she took the lid off, I knew the black leather jacket that lay on top was Jade the Tyrant's jacket.

"Well, try it on," she urged.

The jacket fitted well.

"There's no tag on the back so you can wear it around London without fear. I'd be honoured if you'd take it."

"Let me see it on you first?" I said.

"No chance. You might catch me wearing jeans now and again, but I won't be wearing leather again."

"It looks good on you," Dad said, as he stood in the doorway studying me.

As he rummaged inside the box, I stood behind him and looked over his shoulder at his memories. Concert tickets, newspaper reports, photos, and there was even a drumstick signed by Nicko, from Iron Maiden, my favourite rock band.

"How come you guys didn't have a tag?" I asked. "I thought all gangs wore patches."

"Who said we didn't have a tag?" Dad answered. "When I met your mum, we had our name printed on the back of the jackets. Later, we changed it to the Tyrants' tag. I removed the symbol from the jacket the same night the Tyrants disbanded."

Dad reached down into the box again, took out a small black jewellery box and gave it to me. Inside was a man's silver, signet ring. The black, quartz, square displayed an icon similar to the symbol for peace.

"I gave your mum an identical ring while she was in the hospital recovering from a knife wound. Every member of the Tyrants wore this ring. You have Jade's jacket, I want you to have Marcus's ring. But you have to promise you'll never wear it."

"I can't, it's too big," I joked.

"You have no idea what would happen if you displayed the Tyrant's tag around London," he continued.

"I know all about it," I assured him. "Clay and Beth filled me in. Don't worry; I'm not even using my real name in public. I promise I won't wear it. Thanks, Dad. You never really wanted to forget, did you?" I looked into their faces. "You kept these treasures locked up, hoping they would stay hidden forever, but you kept them because you couldn't let go completely. Could you?"

"No. I suppose not," Mum said, walking over to Dad. She put her arm around his waist and leaned onto his arm.

"I had the best and worst life experiences as a member of the Tyrants, and it's not an easy thing to forget."

He looked down at her and then kissed her; as though he was kissing Jade the teenager. I think they forgot about me being in the room.

I coughed. "Umm, so we're okay now?"

"Yeah," she said, and then looked up at him and smiled. Turning, she faced me. "I'm not saying we're going to start blasting rock music from open windows, but I promise to relax and loosen up a little."

"Don't expect too much," Dad added. "It will take time."

I stood up and walked toward the door.

"Please call Clay and Beth, they miss you guys so much."

"Promise," Mum called.

I left them to it. I used to get embarrassed when my parents were affectionate with one another, but because I knew the truth about the relationship, the heartache and tragedy they'd gone through, seeing their love warmed my heart.

***

I was helping them prepare dinner, when I decided to mention the band.

"I was thinking of taking a ride down to the Thistle, before dinner, to see if they're interested in having the band come down and give a free performance."

"Perfect place for a band named ChainMail," Mum said, her sarcasm getting the better of her.

"Isn't it a long way to come, especially when you're not getting paid?" Dad asked, as he took his time peeling the potatoes.

"The performance is for you guys. If the mountain won't come to Mohamed. Actually, I was thinking of ringing around to see if I can get some more gigs. You know, make a mini tour out of it. Would it be okay if I stayed for a few days if I get something set up?"

I grabbed a piece of carrot before Mum could throw them into the boiling water.

"Of course," she answered. "It will be nice to have you home."

"The house seems empty without John," Dad said.

It was the first time either of them had mentioned his name.

I swallowed the carrot and then coughed. "I know it still hurts, but we can talk about him, you know."

My eyes started watering as the carrot got stuck in my throat. Mum patted by back.

"I was saving the ring for John," Dad said, somber.

I gulped down a glass of water, trying to hide the embarrassment of my choking fit.

"Well then the ring means even more to me now. I miss him a lot. You know the situation with Tania messed him up big time. Finding out the truth about Dylan was just the icing on the cake. If he wasn't depressed before then, I'm sure we could have talked this out."

"You know, it's the first time I heard you say Dylan's name," Mum said. Her eyes glazed over and I could almost see her memories.

"It won't be the last time either," I declared. "I might not have had the chance to meet him, but I would like to know him, if one day you're ready to talk. So who's coming for a ride down to the Thistle?"

"You've got to be joking, on that heap." Mum laughed.

"Hey, that's my baby," I declared.

Dad looked out of the window and nodded to my bike. "Clay did the paint job didn't he? I'd recognize his work anywhere."

"Yeah, he fixed her up good," I said.

"So, Dad, will I be seeing you in jeans when you come to hear the band?"

He laughed. "I doubt it, but we'll see."

"Okay, I'm off. I'll be back before dinner. Are you sure I can't tempt you with a quick pint?"

"Maybe later." Mum smiled.

***

I wanted the Thistle gig to be one of the best yet. This was for my parents, and I wanted to make them proud. I never mentioned to the guys that they were going to be playing for free. I didn't think they'd go for it, and so I paid for their time myself.

We set up the band equipment late that afternoon. I'd bought some material, which looked similar to chain mail, and used it to decorate the top of the stage. With our black banner displayed at the back of the stage, the set up looked mean. I knew Mum and Dad would be impressed. I made sure the landlord advertised the gig a week in advance. The last thing I needed was my parents to turn up to an empty house. Boy would that deflate my ego.

I stayed around the back with Todd, Greg, and Jake while the pub filled up. I guess I was a little nervous about performing in front of my parents, but the dope helped me to relax.

I didn't want to give my folks a fright, and strip off on stage, so I wore tight, black jeans and a plum, velvet corset. I dressed up my hair with a dark brown, clip-on hair piece that gave the impression of body and length. I thought I looked sexy and tough.

As soon as we walked on stage, I searched the audience to see if I could spot them. I almost didn't recognize them. Mum had died her hair back to its original colour. If it were longer, she would have looked just like the red head in the Tyrant photo. She was wearing blue jeans and a black T-shirt. Dad was still wearing trousers, but at least he made the effort and wore a causal T-shirt. Both had a pint of beer in front of them. It was the first time I'd seen them with a drink, and it brought a big smile to my face. I blew them a kiss.

"Evening everyone," I announced over the mike. "We're ChainMail and we're thrilled to have you here." I paused until the cheers died down. "I'm dedicating tonight's performance to two very special people. Jade and Marcus, this is for you."

Mum and Dad's face lit up, as Todd strummed the intro to "Sweet Child of Mine".

I didn't have a chance to speak with my parents until after the show. After two encores, I finally left the stage and sat down with them.

"That was awesome!" Dad said.

"I had no idea you were so talented," Mum said with pride.

I was beaming. The audience was appreciative and a great crowd to perform for. The landlord wanted to book us again and begged us to reconsider. I told him the gig was a one off, but if I were down that way again, I'd give him a call. We had three more gigs in Birmingham and my folks went to every one. They couldn't get enough of ChainMail.

At each gig, I was given a glimpse of the real Jade and Marcus. Mum would sit swaying and nodding to the rhythm as she sang along. And she surprised me by knowing all the words to the Heart and Iron Maiden songs. She really got into it. Dad shocked me when I saw him happily chatting away to a group of bikers standing by the bar. You can't imagine how much it meant to me to see them being their true selves and accepting me for who I was.

CHAPTER SIX

My reunion with Buzz was one that made me swear I wouldn't be parted from him again. I didn't realize how much I missed him until I was back in his arms. He wouldn't leave my side, and was openly affectionate to me in front of the Wolves. Not in a vulgar way as he did before; marking his territory, displaying to the pack that he owned me, and I would do anything he said. He was considerate and loving; it was a side of Buzz I hadn't seen before. Against my better judgement, I was falling in love with him.

I knew he wanted me, sexually. I couldn't understand why he never tried to take it further. I thought women were supposed to be the ones who played hard to get. Was it that he didn't like the act of sexual intercourse, or was he just using me for foreplay? One month on, and I was seriously questioning my sexual appeal.

I saw Buzz nearly every night. He'd pick me up somewhere, or we'd meet after my gig. Then we'd go for a ride, park up, and fool around. However, he always took me back to my bike. I'd yet to spend the night.

Then on a Tuesday evening, we were around his place, and had decided to stay in for the night. Around eight thirty, he left to get a Chinese takeaway.

Buzz's apartment was small. One bedroom, bathroom, open kitchen and small lounge; modern in décor with grey painted walls, chocolate coloured door frames, and stylish silver and glass cabinets and table. My eyes locked on his music system, and as I went to check it out, I tripped over the edge of the blue shag rug that covered most of the tiled floor. The plasma TV was also top of the range. Like all the rest, it impressed me, but didn't surprise. What with the amount of money he was likely making from the Wolves' illegal activities, he could afford the best.

Buzz didn't live in a bad part of the East end, but then again, the apartment wasn't on a rich estate either. The district suited his needs, I supposed. Close enough to the clubhouse, his brothers, and any action.

The apartment was tidy for a bachelor, but that wasn't surprising since he hardly stayed there, preferring to crash at a Wolf's house or spend the night with a woman. Oh, yeah, he told me exactly how it was. But I didn't feel jealous. If he was playing around, at least I was getting more of his time than Mandy or the others were. I hoped he'd been spending more evenings at home since meeting me. I hoped, but I doubted it.

Feeling restless, I went into the kitchen and stood by the beige twin sink, while I washed up glasses and some coffee mugs. I wanted Buzz to see what he was getting, that if he stuck with me, he'd be looked after in every capacity.

I heard the front door open and close and the sound of plastic bags being put on the kitchen table. The aroma of crispy duck wafted past my nose.

Buzz crept up behind me and grabbed me around the waist. He was soaked, and from the manly scent, I knew it wasn't raining outside.

His wet T-shirt pressed against my back and his sweaty cheek nuzzled my neck.

I turned and took an intake of breath.

His hair was dripping from sweat; his cheek held a red welt and his lip was bleeding.

"What the hell happened to you?" I gasped.

"Ssh," he said, putting his finger to my lip.

His knuckles were cut and bleeding as well.

I opened my mouth and sucked at his finger. I knew he wasn't in the mood for talking.

Reaching down with his other hand, he lifted up my skirt. His sweaty skin and scent were tuning me on. Whoever found the other end of Buzz's fist, sure gave my man a good workout.

He picked me up and carried me into the bedroom. His panting and groaning as I licked and kissed him told me he was just as excited as I was about the next phase.

I wanted to ask him why now? Why had he waited so long? But I kept my questions to myself, closed my eyes, and enjoyed every orgasm he gave me.

God, I knew making love to Buzz was going to be something special. He was experienced, knew what I wanted, which buttons to press. I thought the first time would be just wild sex. It never occurred to me he might be a considerate lover. He told me how much my body excited him, and that he loved a curvy woman. He was dominating at times, ordering me into different positions, and grabbing my legs to open or bend them further.

After three hours of kisses, foreplay, and intercourse, we lay beside one another while our naked bodies glistened and dripped with sweat.

I was silently giving myself a score for my performance and wondering what Buzz would score me as, when he turned his back to me.

"I think it's best if we don't see each other again."

My score went from a nine to zero.

Was I that bad? I pulled him onto his back. He was going to have to face me if he was dumping me.

I stared at him. I didn't know what to say. We'd just spent hours making love, and I was sure he was satisfied, and then he threw me away. Maybe that was the way he treated all his women. What made his full time woman special? What did Mandy have that I didn't?

"You're a nice girl and shouldn't be anywhere near the Wolves or me," he said.

"Where's this coming from? Did I do something wrong? Am I not good enough?"

"Shit, Dior, it's not that. If things were different. A different time and place, I probably wouldn't let you out of my sight. But you're too good for this lifestyle and me."

"Fuck, not you as well, I've had this shit from my friends. Buzz, I know what I want, and it's you." I caressed his cheek, but he sat up and started to dress.

"You don't know what the fuck you want. And you don't know shit about me. There's nothing exciting about being a Wolf. And associating with one will cause you nothing but trouble."

"But surely that's my decision to make?" I argued.

There was no way I was allowing him to walk away. I was so close. I had him where I wanted, and now he was pulling away. I know he was warning me off. I had an idea of what I was willingly going to experience. What I didn't realize is what I would be getting unwillingly.

He shook his head "You're not listening to me. I don't want to see you again. Leave here, go home, and don't look back."

"Buzz, don't do this, please. We can carry on seeing each other. The Wolves don't need to be involved," I lied. "I need you, not them."

"I'm a Wolf," he yelled. "You can't have one without the other. I'm an outlaw biker. I have a record. I'm a drug dealer. I carry a gun. I've fucked more cunts than I care to remember. Do you get it now?"

He walked out without another word. The door slammed shut and I wept into the sheet as his words echoed through my head.

He'd given it to me straight; told me who he was and what life as a Wolf was going to be like. Half of me wanted to run back home, only then I remembered why I was in London in the first place. It wasn't to fall in love; it wasn't to become a member of the Wolves.

I had been sidetracked. I hadn't given much thought to where and how I was supposed to pull off my stupidly daring achievement, but I knew my need for revenge must take precedence over any emotions I felt for Buzz.

***

I carried on working hard at my job and singing most evenings just to get my mind off him. I assumed he would call.

I searched the faces in the pubs I played, and although I recognized a couple of the Wolves, Buzz never showed. I left it a week before hunting him down.

The Drunken Squid was their local, and the clubhouse was on the outskirts of town. Clay had taught me a lot about the biker code, and I knew it would be dangerous to go walking into the clubhouse without an invite. The Drunken Squid was the best choice. Hey, I'm a biker, I can go into a bikers' pub and have a pint anytime I like, and it just happens the pub was the Wolves' regular haunt. It wasn't as though it was the first time I'd been there.

Anyone who walked into the Drunken Squid would know immediately it was a bikers' bar. Walls were covered with biker memorabilia: flags, T-shirts, banners, and posters. Décor left a lot to be desired, but it didn't matter what the place looked like, as long as the beer was cold and the music was loud and hard.

Dressed in a short, black denim skirt, off the shoulder top, and stiletto boots, I took my Harley and rode down to the pub. I counted seventeen motorbikes out front. God knows how many were parked around the back.

There was a good chance Buzz was there. I just wished it wasn't so crowded. I knew I looked good and would get plenty of attention. However, the only one I wanted to be attentive was Buzz.

I walked inside the pub and made straight for the bar. There were only four bikers present, which made me wonder why there were so many bikes outside. I bought a beer and then sat alone at a small, round, scratched varnished table. I'd been sitting there for five minutes when a biker came into the room via the lounge door. I heard laughter and music coming from the next room, as the door swung shut.

I watched him leaning over the bar as he spoke to the barman.

The Wolf's patch was evident.

Turning his head, his eyes lit up, and he made a beeline straight for me.

"Hey babe. You on your own?" he asked.

"Looks like it, doesn't it."

"We're having a private party around the back, why don't you come and join in."

"Is Buzz around?" I asked.

The biker appeared surprised, and then a look of recognition crossed his face. "You're the singer ain't you? Yeah, he's in the back. You want me to get him?"

"Just give him a message. Tell him Dior's in the bar."

"Sure you don't want to want to give him the message yourself? You're welcome to join the party."

I didn't like the way the guy was staring at my legs. "No thanks. I'm fine here."

The Wolf shrugged and then walked away.

Buzz turned up a few minutes later. It seemed ages since I'd last seen him, and I forgot how sexy the man was. I smiled at him, but the smile wasn't returned.

"What the fuck are you doing here?" he whispered. "I warned you to stay away. You don't know what the hell you're getting yourself into." He turned his head and looked toward the lounge door.

I stood up and touched his arm.

"Look at me, Buzz. Tell me you don't want me. Tell me to leave and I will, but I know that's not how you feel."

"You shouldn't have come here, Dior. You should have left things as they were. We had a good time, that's all. You're a great lay, but you're not good enough. I don't want you."

He was blunt and gave it to me straight, but his eyes said differently.

I put my hand around the back of his neck and kissed his lips. I pushed myself close to him until I could feel how much he wanted me.

He stopped the embrace, and gripped hold of my shoulders.

"If this is what you really want, I can't stop you. You're in over your head. Just don't say I didn't warn you. I'm not going to be responsible for what happens."

Grabbing hold of my hand, we left the room and walked into the lounge.

The party was in full swing. The room was full of leather and patches. Loud rock music played in the background while the bikers attempted to talk over the volume. The place was crowded and noisy.

I kept my head down as Buzz dragged me through the deluge of drunken Wolves. As he stopped to chat,

I turned and saw Mandy trying to make her way over. Pulling on his arm, I got his attention and informed him of the approaching trouble. He leaned forward, whispered to his friend, and then pushed his way through to the back of the lounge. I turned my head around and just caught a glimpse of the Wolf cutting her off and standing as a barrier while she tried to get to us.

Buzz opened a door to a private office and pulled me inside.

"Shit, that was close," I laughed.

Pushing me up against the wall, he pulled off my jacket, grabbed at my top, and sucked on my neck. Man I was horny. I wanted him bad.

Lifting my leg up, I wrapped it around his bum and pulled him closer. His erection pressed into me and my stomach quivered. His hand slowly made his way up to the top of my thigh and then under the skirt. Just as his finger started probing, the office door opened.

I tried to bring my leg down, but Buzz kept hold of it. I took a quick look at the biker standing by the door and then buried my red face into Buzz's neck.

Not once did Buzz turn and address the biker. Still sucking and kissing my breasts, he asked him what he wanted.

"The guys were just wondering… you know. If there was going to be any entertainment?"

"When I'm done," Buzz answered.

Once I heard the door shut, I checked that the biker had gone and then grabbed Buzz's hair and forced his head up. I kissed him fiercely, biting his lip and sucking his tongue. Then I reached down and squeezed him. He jolted from the pain, but I wanted it to hurt. I knew we were going to have animal sex, and I was ready for it. Well, I thought I was.

He took me from behind and naive as I was, I didn't know what he was about to do. It felt wrong and yet exciting.

"It's okay, just relax," he told me in a husky voice.

Buzz grabbed hold of my hair and started rocking. Each rock pushed him deeper inside. The rhythm increased, and I could feel myself loosening up. I had never had an orgasm like it. My whole body quaked and quivered. The sensations were nothing like I'd ever experienced; total weakness.

I was still panting and out of breath, when I bent down to retrieve my knickers. Buzz dressed and then walked around the back of the desk and sat in the chair.

He gazed at me and then motioned for me to sit on the chair opposite him.

"You hang around with the Wolves, you become their property. You do what they say, when they say it, or suffer the consequences. If you're regarded as a beneficial member, someone who brings something into the club, then you get to wear the Lady tag. But women are always thought of as seconds. You will never be respected, you will never go up in rank, and you will never wear the Wolf patch on your jacket. You understand what I'm saying Dior? I'm giving you one last chance to walk away."

"Tell me you don't want me, and I'm out the door," I said.

"Shit, it's not that. You're different from other women and that's why I don't want to see you get hurt. You're naive and weak, but that'll change. If you hang out with the Wolves, you'll harden. You'll have to get tough, and I won't be holding your hand. You'll have to defend yourself, and I don't think you're strong enough for that."

"I appreciate your vote of confidence, Buzz. I'll be fine. I can take care of myself. You have no idea how capable I am. I've made up my mind."

Buzz frowned and shook his head.

"I can walk away anytime I like, can't I?" I asked.

"Yes. But once you get your colours it'll be harder."

"Then what are you worrying about? If I can't take the pace, I'll walk away, and you will never see me again. Okay?"

"Nothing I say is going to change your mind is it?"

"Nope," I said.

He stood up. "You want a drink?"

"Man, you've just read my mind."

I went to stand, but he pushed me back onto the chair.

"No, I'll get them. You wait here."

I stayed seated and watched him leave. Boy I wanted to celebrate. I got this far. Inside the Wolves' den, and one step closer to my goal—revenge.

Buzz came back a few minutes later and handed me a cold bottle of beer. My thirst was such, I guzzled the beer straight down.

"I like to see a woman who enjoys a drink." He smiled tightly.

"Yeah, well, I worked up a thirst. So, you got shares in this place or what?" I asked, as I looked over the office.

As well as the desk, a grey filing cabinet covered the sidewall. Files and books lined the shelves, and I couldn't help but notice the threadbare couch that was pushed into the far corner of the room.

"Use that much?" I smirked.

"Yeah, and I'm going to be using it now."

He pulled me up and led me over to the couch. Taking off my top and bra, he then stripped me of my skirt and pants. I stood naked and shameless in front of him. He walked over to the wall and dimmed the lights. Perfect setting, I thought. The room was starting to spin, and I blamed it on drinking the beer too fast. Then my vision blurred. Buzz laid me down on the couch. I couldn't focus on his face, but I saw his shadow walk away. I wanted to call out to him, but I had no control over my voice. My mouth opened, but nothing came out. I felt as though I was floating away…

I woke up as a shower of cool water hit my face. Buzz was standing beside me holding me up. The water was pouring into my mouth. I spluttered and I struggled to move, but he forced me to stay where I was. I felt sleepy and didn't realize what was going on.

"What you doing?" I asked.

"Just cleaning you up. It's okay. You feel alright?"

His voice was gentle sounding, as though he was talking to a frightened child. Was I ill? I wondered.

The water stopped running and a warm fluffy towel was wrapped around me. Holding me around the waist, he walked me out of the bathroom, back into the bedroom and laid me on the bed.

Still disorientated, the pain didn't register.

Buzz sat on the edge of the bed, watching me. I smiled. His returned smile looked strained. Brushing away a strand of wet hair from my check, he then bent down and kissed my forehead, and then taking his boots off, laid on the bed beside me. I remember feeling very weak and tired. My eyes closed, just as Buzz whispered. "I'm going to make it up to you."

I woke up the following morning with a terrible hangover. My head was pulsating and my stomach felt queasy. I knew I hadn't drunk a lot, so I couldn't understand why I was feeling like I was.

As I sat up, the pain between my legs made me cry out. It felt like someone had taken a razor blade and cut me. I needed to pee and so moved to the edge of the bed and put my feet down onto the corded carpet

A movement in the corner of the room caught my eye. The cream blinds allowed just enough sunlight into the room for me to see Buzz sitting on an armchair in the far corner of the room. His arms were folded and he was staring at me.

I knew he was giving me attitude. I wondered why, but didn't have time to ask. I needed the toilet. I tried to keep the urine inside, but I could already feel it running down my leg. The stinging sensation was unbearable. I ran into the bathroom in tears. I assumed I caught something from Buzz. But I'd never had an STD before, so I had no idea what the symptoms were. It wasn't until I was able to get off the toilet and move to the sink, that I knew something was very wrong.

Red handprints covered my neck. My lip was cut and my right eye was bruised.

I cursed at my reflection. Buzz stood in the doorway.

I turned and faced him. "What the fuck happened?"

"You wanted to get in with the Wolves, so you got what every piece of fresh meats gets."

"And what's that?"

"Babe, you were fucked front and back. You were last night's entertainment."

"I was what!"

"You were a participant in a Wolves' gang bang."

"I was raped?"

I felt sick and thought I was going to pass out. Everything made sense; the pain between my legs, the headache and sickness.

"I wouldn't call it rape. I never heard you say no," he sniggered.

"You were there? You saw it happen and you didn't do anything?" I screamed.

I couldn't believe what I was hearing.

"Hell, I knew. Why do you think I spiked your drink? I didn't want you to know what was happening. I warned you. I gave you a chance to walk away."

"You never fucking said my initiation would be a gang-banging," I cried.

"It's a rule of the Wolves. All new pieces of arse get a good going over. You think I wanted to stand and watch them do that to you? I didn't get any pleasure in it, I assure you. I wanted to make sure they didn't hurt you. A few of them like it rough.

"Hey, you got off easy. I've never bothered drugging a newbie before. They're fucked whether they like it or not. The ones that take it end up as someone's property after everyone has had a go; the ones that can't don't come back. Most of them know what to expect when they walk in. Those that don't, well they soon learn."

"You bastard." I screamed.

I swung my fist but he caught me by the arm. I struggled, wanting to rip the bastard apart.

He was laughing, which enraged me even more.

"You're lucky the women didn't have a go cause the guys love a good lesbian show."

I couldn't take any more. Exhausted in body, mind, and spirit, I crumpled to the floor.

Buzz stood where he was for a moment, and then he knelt down beside me.

"If it's any consolation, it won't happen again. I'll make sure of that."

"It shouldn't have happened at all," I cried. "Why did you allow them to rape me in the first place?"

"I told you. Any woman who walks into the pack is played. I couldn't stop it."

"But you're the president. They have to listen to you."

"I'm acting president, V.P, but the title means shit. I could be voted out any time. I have to abide by the code just like the rest of them."

I had no energy left to argue with him.

Picking me up in his arms, he carried me back into

the bedroom. I hated him, but I still wanted him, and I hated myself for wanting him.

Laying me on the bed, he sat on the edge, his head turned away.

I grabbed his arm and swung him around to face me. "How many?"

"I wasn't counting. Whoever wanted a go. You had many admirers."

"That's why you… You knew they were going to take me …"

Looking me straight in the eye, his face showed no shame or regret "Yes. I knew. I wanted you ready. "

"You fucking bastard," I whispered.

His face turned red and his eyes blackened as he stood up.

"Fuck you, Dior," he spat. "You wanted in. You wouldn't fucking listen to me. Take your medicine bitch!"

He stormed out of the apartment slamming the door behind him.

I spent the rest of the morning in bed, feeling used, hurt, dirty, and embarrassed. I was angry with myself for not listening to him. He did try to warn me, and he gave me plenty of opportunity to walk away. Maybe I deserved what I got.

But then again, he could have told me what would have happened if I stayed. He could have given me the choice. I would have walked. Nothing, not even my immense desire for revenge was worth that. I would have found another way to fuck the Wolves without fucking the Wolves. Those bastards were going to pay. I was going to get my own back for what they did to me.

It was late in the afternoon when Buzz showed his face again. He didn't bring me flowers, chocolates, or an apology. Just a chemist bag, which he threw onto my lap.

"Are you okay?" He asked.

What a fucking question to ask. "Well, I haven't slit my wrists if that's what you're asking," I snapped.

"Have you told anyone about what happened? Did you call the police?" He demanded.

"Is that all you're fucking worried about? Screw you. I don't have anyone to call, as well you know. And you made sure you washed away any evidence of the rape. I deserved what happened to me; at least that's what the police would say. Fuck, I walked into a den of animals; the Wolves, a perfect name for you. I should have known better, but I stupidly thought you'd be looking out for me."

"They would have had you anyway," he said. "They would have raped and then beaten you when you tried to fight them off, I've seen it happen too many times. Hell, I've done it myself. A least with the drug I gave you, you didn't know what was happening."

"Oh yeah, sure, that makes it all better. Fuck, Buzz. I was raped, and you allowed it to happen. And what the hell is this?" I screamed, pointing to my swollen eye.

"Shit, Dior, there was nothing I could do to stop it from happening. They had to have their turn. It's how it works."

"So now I'm their property, and they can take me any time they want?"

"No. It won't happen again. If you still want in, I'll make sure no one touches you."

"Yeah, like they're gonna fucking listen to you."

"When a Wolf takes a female member for himself, he marks her as his property. You've seen the jackets they wear. The established females are referred to as someone's Lady and the white lettering across the back of the jacket informs other members they're not to be touched. Dior, you have to understand I could have been kicked out if I refused you to them."

"What makes you think your word will hold rank now?" I asked.

"They had their go, now you're mine. I own you and they can't touch you."

I thought about what he said. I wasn't so hot about the idea of anyone owning me, but knowing I wouldn't be hurt by the Wolves again, eased my anxiety a little.

"What about what's-her-name… she's not going to like this?"

"Yeah, that's a problem you'll have to sort out; and soon. But it's your problem. Mandy's not going to let you walk in and take over her position without a fight."

I sighed. "Why does it have to be so difficult? All I wanted to do was to join your little club and be with you."

He smiled and I smiled back.

"Do you want to go for a ride, get some fresh air?" He asked.

"No. I'm not going anywhere. I can't fucking walk. My arse is still bleeding and my face is a mess, as if you didn't know."

"What the hell do you want me to say?" he yelled. "I got you out of there in one piece; I drugged you so you wouldn't know what was happening. I watched over you and looked after you last night."

"What do you want, fucking gratitude?"

'I didn't do it for gratitude. Look, get some rest, I'll sleep over at a friend's house. You can stay here as long as you like. You know where to find me."

"You're going to her, aren't you?" I yelled.

"Nah, I'll fuck something else. There's plenty on offer for a Wolf."

He made it outside, just as the glass I threw shattered on the door.

CHAPTER SEVEN

I had to get tough. If I was going to make it through this in one piece, if I was ever going to wear their fucking colours and get the inside info I needed, I had to learn how to fight. I needed to take care of Mandy and until that happened, I would never be accepted by the rest of the pack. In truth, I couldn't give a flying fuck what the others thought of me, but I had a plan, and that included getting chummy with those mother fuckers.

I'd been in fights at school, but nothing real violent and vicious. What I didn't know was how good a fighter Mandy was.

There was only one person I could turn to, and that was Clay. He wasn't surprised when I told him I was having some trouble and needed to sort someone out.

"Comes with the territory," he said.

I never mentioned my association with the Wolves or what had happened to me. I didn't want him involved.

Clay taught me how to defend myself against fists and weapons. He taught me how and where to punch to cause damage. I trained hard and worked up a sweat in every session. I was building up my confidence as well as my muscles. I knew I couldn't walk back into the Drunken Squid without being ready. But I didn't want to leave it too long. I hadn't seen him for a week. I didn't want him to think I had changed my mind and walked away, even though if I had any sense, I should have done just that. I was going to show him and the rest of the dogs that I wasn't to be messed with, and I had the right to wear their colours.

I tried my talent out on an unsuspecting female punter, one night after I'd finished a gig.

I'd been watching her most of the evening. Every sour face and dirty look she pulled wound me up even more. By the time I left the stage, I was raging.

"Did you see that fucking tart out there," I yelled at Todd.

"Just let it go," he said.

"No way. I'm not having any bitch dissing me."

"What's with the attitude?" Jake asked.

"What do you expect? Look who she hangs with." Greg scowled.

I pushed past them and went back into the bar. She was still there, but standing up with her coat on her arm ready to leave. I leant against the bar and stared at her. She left with two other women.

I didn't have a problem with the other two, but I was ready to take the lot of them on if I had too. I'd never felt anger like that before. My hands were itching; I felt a burning sensation crawling up my arms. My heart was racing and my stomach was in knots. I followed them outside and then called out.

"Hey. I want a word with you."

I was still wearing my costume of velvet corset, tight P.V.C trousers, and black patent stilettos.

The women quickened their pace.

I ran up to the one that had been giving me the looks, grabbed her arm and swung her around. Without giving her a moment to defend herself, my fist flew out and punched her in the face. She staggered back but didn't go down. The other two stepped toward me.

"Don't even think about it," I warned.

One ran off toward the bar. The other dived into her bag, took her mobile out, and then ran off.

"You think I'm going to allow you to diss me like that in public. You've no fucking idea who I run with." I screamed at the bitch.

I punched her again, this time in the stomach. Not once did she try to fight back. It was a good job as well; otherwise I wouldn't have stepped away.

Guys came running out of the bar shouting. One grabbed my arms and pinned them behind my back, the other two went to the woman's aid.

"She just attacked me," the woman cried through short breaths.

I went ballistic, and started kicking and screaming, fighting to get out of his grasp so I could finish the bitch off.

"Get the fuck off me!" I screamed, and then head butted the guy behind me.

"Dior, for Christ's sake,"

I turned around to see Greg helping Todd, whose nose was pouring with blood. I had no idea he was the one restraining me.

"You're out of control," Jake growled.

"I think you'd better find another band to play with," Greg added, "I don't want you around anymore."

"Fuck you," I yelled.

I started to walk over to my bike when Todd called out.

"Dior. Get out before it's too late." His voice sounded muffled, and although unclear, I heard and understood what he said.

Stupidly, I thought I didn't need them, that I didn't need anyone. For a second the thought worried me. After a short association with the Wolves, I was already changing. Changing into someone I wouldn't like. The thought was quickly eaten up my anger.

It would have been the ideal time to go down to The Drunken Squid and have it out with Mandy, but I needed to calm down. Clay said that too much rage was a bad thing.

What I needed was a joint. Climbing onto my bike, I rode off, not caring that I wasn't wearing my jacket or helmet. I never returned to the pub to collect my things, and I never heard from Jake, Todd, and Greg again.

***

I didn't plan on the time and day I was going to go down to the Drunken Squid for the show down with Mandy. It just happened.

I was on my way back to Clay and Beth's from an audition, when some jerk in a red pickup truck, pulled out and smashed into the front of my bike.

I came off and landed hard on my side. I wasn't worried about myself; I was more concerned about my ride. I got off the ground and ran over to check the damage. Okay, it wasn't a brand new Harley or anything, but she was my baby, and I'd yet to have an accident on her.

The guy was just stepping out of the truck when I went up to him. Deciding it was probably safer inside; he jumped back in.

I banged on the side of the driver's door, hard enough to get his attention.

"What the fuck was that?" I screamed.

Holding up his hands defensively, he yelled back. "Didn't you see me indicating?"

"Didn't you see me coming along side of you?" I shouted back "Get out, so we can sort this out."

He shook his head.

Up until then, I was actually calm. However, the moment he refused to step out of the truck, my rage mounted.

"Get out of the fucking truck," I warned.

He then had the nerve to push the door lock down.

"You son of a bitch," I yelled. "Open the fucking door." I grabbed hold of the handle and pulled. My rage was such, I swear I could have pulled the door off, if it wasn't for the guy putting the truck in gear and driving off.

I screamed at him and watched his truck drive away before turning my attention back to my bike.

The silver fender was dented, and the left front light was just hanging on, the glass was shattered. There wasn't a lot of damage; it was the fact that there shouldn't have been any damage in the first place which pissed me off.

The guy had left the scene without giving me any of his details, not that there was a lot that could be fixed. I'd get Clay to hammer out the dent, but the damage would always be there, in my mind. He may have gotten away with it, but I knew who was going to pay. I started up my bike and headed straight for the Drunken Squid.

It had been nearly a week and a half since I last saw Buzz. And he looked even better for it.

His face was expressionless when he noticed me. However Mandy, who was sitting on a stool beside him, looked surprised to see me again.

There were around fifteen bikers inside. If I was going to get any respect from them, I would have to give them a good show, and be victorious. I walked up to where they were both sitting and ignored the stares that followed me. Standing beside their table, I glared down at her.

"You and me, outside, now." I wanted enough room to swing a punch into her smug face and didn't like the idea of smashing into the pub furniture.

My stomach was in knots, my fists clenched ready.

She stood up and faced me. "Yeah, if you're ready to be taught some fucking manners, let's finish this."

Any other time, her tough mouth would have scared me. But the way I was feeling that moment, the rage that was flowing through me increased with every black stare she gave. She walked past me and headed for the back exit.

I bent down to Buzz, grabbed hold of his balls, and then whispered in his ear, "I'll deal with you later."

As I walked away smiling, chatter in the bar erupted. Squeaking chairs informed me that the Wolves were following. An outsider taking on a Lady Wolf was a fight they weren't going to miss.

The back of the pub was fenced, away from prying eyes, and as most of the bikes were parked around the front, there was plenty of room to throw a punch.

I walked over to where she stood waiting. The bikers circled around us.

"You have two choices," I said. "You can either walk back inside, find yourself another dick to suck on, or we fight this out and the loser doesn't show her face around here again."

Both our heads turned to Buzz. He nodded.

"Agreed," she said. "You think you're the first skank to walk in the den and try to take my man and position. You're gonna get what everyone of those bitches got."

"Maybe," I said, "but the difference is I'm going to be the one walking back inside."

She ran at me swinging a punch. From the way it was directed, I thought she was aiming for my face, so I raised my hands to protect myself. The blow landed in my stomach. As I doubled up, her knee smashed my chin.

The fight had only just begun, and I was already on the dusty ground, spiting blood.

I knew she was tough. I just didn't realize how tough, until I felt her first punch. Oohs and curses came from the Wolves, while the women screamed encouragement to Mandy.

Lying on the ground winded, I tried coughing up my breath. I rubbed my chin, but knew she hadn't done any real damage because I could still move my jaw.

The women's yells suddenly stopped, as though they had been cut off. I looked up at Buzz. He didn't have to say anything. His expression was willing me to get up. I wasn't about to let him or myself down.

I stayed where I was, discretely keeping a watch on Mandy. Then when she came closer, I grabbed her ankles and threw her to the ground. Sitting on her stomach, I allowed my rage to take over. My fist punched her face while the other hand held her down. A wisp of hair across my face and I stopped punching to sweep it away. Mandy reached out and grabbed my throat. I used my elbow to whack her in the face, but it took three blows before she let go. Her grip left me choking and gasping for air.

We were both hurting, but neither was ready to surrender defeat. Still on the ground, we rolled around in the dirt and dust punching any part of each other's body that we could.

Exhausted, I stopped and lay back, panting. Mandy did the same. I wanted to see if she wanted more punishment, so I pushed myself off the ground and turned towards her.

Her right eye was cut and starting to swell. Her nose was bleeding and her bottom lip was split. She looked a mess and I felt satisfied.

I stood up and bent over to catch my breath when I noticed her getting up. A few seconds later a knife came swishing past my chest. It just missed me. I cursed for not knowing any better. Looking to the Wolves, I silently urged them to give me a blade. Not one hand reached for their back pockets.

Mandy was dancing around as though wired on drugs; I knew if she got the chance, she would have cut me open. She ran at me with the knife out stretched. Although I dodged every swipe of the blade, I couldn't compete with the weapon. I had to get it away from her.

I tried to grab her wrist but she swiped the knife, the blade sliced through the palm of my hand. Pain didn't register at first. My left hand swung out and punched her in the eye, enabling me this time to grab her wrist and pry the weapon away. The knife dropped to the ground. I kicked it away and then laid into her. My punches were relentless. I only stopped when I became too weak and couldn't lift my hand to throw another punch.

The ground was splattered with a mixture of both our blood. My jeans now dyed red. When I saw the damage to my hand, I knelt in front of her and used the last of my strength to punch her in the side of the face. She went down.

Cheers from the Wolves drowned out my warning to Mandy not to show her face again.

The Wolves congratulated me and told me it was a good fight. They welcomed me back inside. I was hurting, but that didn't wipe the smile off my face.

Back inside, I collapsed in a chair. Tray, the barman, brought me over a cold pint, and I downed it. Buzz sat beside me and forced open my injured hand. Clicking his fingers, he took the bandanna that was offered, and wrapped it tightly around the wound.

"You'll need stitches," he said. "Jem will take you down."

A female Wolf, Lady to Sly, came over and introduced herself as Jem. She wiped away the blood from my face and arms, bathed the wounds with antiseptic lotion, which stung and smelt awful, and then covered them with surgical dressing and plasters.

She was nice, considering a while back she wanted me dead.

Not one of the women shunned me. Everyone came over and made their introductions as they watched Jem cleaning me up. Jem stayed with me at the hospital while I waited in the emergency room until I was seen. I left casualty with a Tetanus shot and seven stitches in my hand.

***

It was nearly two weeks before I could ride my bike again. During that time, I made sure I was a regular at the Drunken Squid. I wanted the Wolves to get to know the real me. I needed their trust.

I couldn't have Buzz picking me up from Clay and Beth's, so I made my own way down to the pub every night, and then taxied home. I told him my relatives would die of shock if they saw us together. Thankfully, he never questioned me further.

It cost a fortune but it was worth the expense. Rather than Clay and Beth finding out I was hanging with the Wolves, or for Buzz to find out I was related to two of the most wanted Tyrants. It was a secret I was determined to keep no matter what.

While I was recuperating, I made sure my man was kept satisfied and didn't go looking elsewhere, or that any new arse would catch his eye. I left an impression on him every night. Boy did that man have a sexual appetite. He needed to get off at least twice a day, sometimes more if I was around. And because of his position in the club, I felt he shouldn't have to initiate or hint when he wanted some. I always made the first move and he never once complained.

I still hadn't brought up the subject of Mud with any of the other Wolves. Buzz mentioned to me that his father was trying to get an early release, but he refused to elaborate. Mud wasn't a subject he liked talking about.

CHAPTER EIGHT

I already had a frog tattoo on my left ankle, a present from Clay and Beth for my nineteenth birthday. So when Buzz wanted me to get another one, I didn't think twice about it, especially as he said he loved seeing tattoos on women, that it made them look like real bikers.

I was a little nervous as we sat in the shop looking through the tattooist's catalogue together. I didn't know if the guy was a licensed tattooist or if his instruments, needles, and such were sterile. The place looked legit and clean, and even though Buzz vouched for the guy, the risk was always in the back of mind.

I ended up choosing a four-pointed star with a sharp, dagger-shaped point. The tattoo started at the top of my right shoulder and went down my arm. The finished design was twelve centimeters in length. I was warned that it would hurt a lot more than my last tattoo, but I wanted to show Buzz how tough I was. Unfortunately, I couldn't put on an act for long. It felt like the guy was dragging a hot knife through my skin. I couldn't prevent the tears that rolled down my face.

Although my arm was sore for about a week, I loved my new tattoo, and because it came from Buzz, it made it even more special. I was a biker and I had tattoos.

Once I was riding again, Buzz invited me on a bike run down to Matlock in Derbyshire. He told me that all the chapters would meet up, and ride down to Matlock together as one convoy, set up a camp, and then party for the weekend. He said it was great way to network and discuss club business with the other officers. Plus, riding in a pack, being seen, kept the Wolves' reputation solid. They went on a run every few months. They lived to ride.

He spoke fervently about what it was like, and what I should expect.

"They'll be a lot of meetings and discussions going on; plenty of drinking, drugs, and women. In fact, once word gets out where we're camping, there'll be skanks queuing up to hang with the Wolves."

I didn't reply.

"You've still got to get your Lady Tag, so although you're treated like a member by the East chapter, the other Wolves will think of you as a prospect. A female prospect gets more shit than a male. You'll be treated like a servant and a sex slave throughout the weekend, and they're gonna love you. You'll be used and abused and no amount of drugging will prepare you for it. I'd rather you stay here than go through that. To tell you the truth, Dior, I've been part of too many gang-bangs and I'm getting sick of them. Only I need you with me. I can't understand it. No one's ever made me feel this way before, and I know it's gonna sound pathetic, but the feeling scares me."

I needed to hear those words. However, the notion that he was falling in love terrified me.

"So, how are we going to get around this?" I asked,

and then kissed his lips. "I don't want to be treated like a prospect, but the run sounds exciting and I'd love to go."

"You've yet to bring anything to the club, so if I called a vote, even though the guys like you, I doubt you'd be tagged. Two abstains and you're out. I don't want to risk a vote until I'm certain. The only way you can come along and not be fucked with, is to come as my guest. No one touches the president's guest. You'll be treated with respect, which is what you deserve. The drawback is you might be told to walk when Wolves' business is discussed. We'll have to keep our distance, act like we're friends rather than lovers."

"Does a guest get to fuck the president?" I asked, gazing into his chocolate coloured eyes.

"Yeah." He grinned. "We'll be together at night. Just don't come on too strong during the day. I'll bring it up at the club's next meeting and warn the chapter to keep their mouths shut about you. I doubt there'll be a problem."

I folded my legs up and laid my head on his lap.

"How many chapters are there?" I asked, as he caressed my hair.

"For now, we're based in London, but I know Mud wants to expand the club. Chosen members would have to move out of London and set up a chapter elsewhere, say Birmingham ..." I swallowed hard. "Then start recruiting new members. There are four chapters. The Mother chapter being us in the East, then we have chapters in the West, North and South of London. Our chapter has about thirty active members."

"Really. I only know about fifteen of them by name."

"Don't worry about it. I don't know all their names either." He laughed.

"There are about a hundred and thirty active Wolves and around twenty prospects, you'll get to meet them on the run."

"What do you mean by active members?" I asked dreamily. His gentle stroke was making me fall asleep.

"They turn up at the club house for regular meetings and party nights. They pay monthly dues, have their own ride, and attend all runs. There's a president, VP, treasurer, accountant and two other officers in each chapter."

I wondered what the two other officers did.

"They're easy to get along with," Buzz continued. "Just watch out for Bee, he can be a mean son of a bitch. He's been trying to get a transfer down to…"

I fell asleep and didn't hear the rest.

***

A small rucksack with a change of clothes, two sleeping bags, and our bikes were all we needed for the Matlock run. Our chapter left the club house with most of its members present. As we rode to each of the houses, more Wolves added to the convoy. We didn't dismount from our bikes at any of the pick up points. The Wolves were ready and waiting. We had a long run and they wanted to get started. Now was not the time for introductions, although I saw more than a few of the Wolves wondering who I was.

We stopped only once to fill up the tanks and get some refreshments. Buzz was smart enough to find a petrol station that had a pub close by. The landlord greeted him and a couple of the other Wolves by name; I figured it was their usual watering hole on the way down to Matlock.

During our stop, I stayed close to the Lady Wolves I knew, so Buzz could chat in private. A couple of bikers made the mistake of trying to hit on me, but Jem soon put them in their place. We stayed for about an hour and half and then hit the road again.

The camp was how I imagined it would be. A large flat area of ground surrounded by woodland trees, which isolated us from the outside and gave us the privacy we wanted. Most of the bikers stayed in their own chapters or grouped up with a few of their brothers around small camp fires. An arrangement of rock songs was playing from numerous stereos. Chatting and laughter filled the air. The Wolves greeted each other like long-lost-friends. Once the bikers were comfortable around their camp fires, Buzz introduced me around to the heads and officers of the other chapters, first as his guest, and then he mentioned I had been the lead singer of ChainMail. Surprisingly, many of the Wolves had heard of the band. My status automatically earned me respect. Buzz was a clever man.

There were more females present than I thought there'd be, and most of them were wary of me. From the way one Lady Wolf was flirting with Buzz, it was obvious they had been more than just casual acquaintances. Buzz noticed me watching, and pushed her away, making it clear he wasn't interested. I turned my head before she caught me looking. I didn't want her to blame me for Buzz's rejection of her. I didn't have any claim on the president, yet he was acting as though I had. I had a difficult time keeping the smile from my face.

I stuck close to the Ladies from our chapter while they introduced me around. I soon felt part of the group, and it was nice to be myself rather than play some role.

The bikers spent half the evening catching up with old friends, while laughter and drink flowed along with the music. Then three of the Wolves lit up the BBQ. The aroma of grilled chicken and sausages soon filed the camp. Once the bikers had their fill, the camp quieted down, the music volume lowered, and everyone sat down around the largest camp fire. I waited for Buzz to give me some indication I shouldn't be there, but he didn't look my way. None of the Wolves looked at me as if to say what are you doing here, take a walk. So I sat between Jem and a Lady called Karen and listened closely to what he had to say.

The discussion wasn't as interesting as I thought it would be. He moaned about late payment of club dues and about an incident that made the paper, involving a robbery. I remember reading about it. Two Wolves were serving time for it.

"Are they being looked after?" Buzz asked the president of their chapter.

"Yeah, no complaints. They have everything they need. There was a small problem, but he was sorted out quickly. Could do with some more leverage though. Our stock is a little low."

Buzz smiled. "I'll sort it. They've earned a holiday."

The club said a prayer, for a fallen Wolf who had died in a bike accident. Then Buzz mentioned about a small group of bikers who were getting themselves known around London. Most of the officers seemed to know who he was referring to, and said they would keep an eye on things and let him know if the group started making too much noise.

"They'll get the shit kicked out of them if they start wearing colours." Buzz said.

I was a surprised they didn't discuss about the gun and drug trafficking that I knew went on, so I assumed they'd talk about that in smaller groups and only with members concerned.

Once the meeting ended, the assembly dispersed back to their smaller camp fires. Several of the Wolves took off on their bikes and then returned two hours later partnered with a woman each.

The women's arrival caused a commotion. The male bikers jumped up, hollered, and cheered.

"Here's the entertainment," Jem whispered.

I wondered if the women knew what they were letting themselves in for, entering a campsite of horny bikers. However, they appeared to relish the attention and didn't seem bothered when the Wolves started feeling them up.

The drugs then came out, I suppose it was to get the women in a relaxed mood, but also so the Wolves could get their nightly fix. Displayed on a folded picnic table, they looked like candies. There were small, plastic boxes containing different shaped, coloured pills, then at least six different types of cannabis in clear plastic bags, white powder, which I assumed was cocaine, and acid stickers; tiny small yellow circles with painted black eyes and a black smile.

I didn't want to take something I didn't know the effect of, worried that I'd get too high or go on a bummer trip and make a fool of myself, so I stuck to grass. I was too embarrassed to ask one of the Wolves what the pills were. I didn't want my cool rep to dissolve.

I'd popped plenty of pills in my time, but it was hard to distinguish what was what. I watched as a handful of the bikers came over to the table and helped themselves to the pick and mix. The grass was strong enough to get me stoned, and on a comfortable high, high enough not to freak out when I came across the orgy.

Buzz looked as though he was having a serious discussion with a couple of the chapter heads and I was feeling bored so I'd decided to go for a walk. What I stumbled upon was more explicit than any porno I'd watched, and it fascinated me.

There were too many naked bodies to count. Sweaty arms and legs entwined, looking like a pile of slithering snakes. To the left of the mound, couples were having sex up against the tree. The woman was being held around her back while she bounced up and down. There didn't seem to be a position that wasn't being tried. To the right, a threesome was going on. It was a shagging feast, and shamefully, the spectacle was turning me on. The grunting, climatic screaming and panting echoed throughout the forest.

I imagine Buzz had joined in with these sex parties. I hoped he was absent because of me.

It didn't look and sound as if the female guests were being forced into doing something they didn't want. In fact, they sounded as though they were enjoying themselves. I felt a little awkward standing there watching. The last thing I wanted was for someone to see me there and invite me to join.

The rest of the Wolves were still partying when I returned. I found Buzz sitting beside Smith, president of the South chapter. I heard laughter so knew I wasn't interrupting anything serious.

Smiling at Smith, I then whispered in Buzz's ear. "I want you, now,"

He stood up and without saying anything to Smith, walked away with me.

I didn't want to have sex too close to the others. I wasn't an exhibitionist, but I was so horny I couldn't wait.

Taking his hand, I led him over to the bikes. I could still see the campsite and people mulling around, but I decided we were far enough not to be noticed.

I pulled Buzz's T-shirt off and then knelt down on the ground and undid his trousers. He didn't say a word, just watched me and pushed my head in a satisfying rhythm. He pulled me up from the ground and kissed me, his tongue exploring my mouth hungrily. Man, I wanted him. I was so hot. I needed him to touch me. I undid the lace on my corset and pulled him to my chest.

I took my jeans off and stood in a black lace thong.

Buzz undressed, then pulled me over to a Wolf's bike.

I felt the tension building up. Buzz was panting hard, I knew he was about to come. His orgasm caused mine to erupt into the longest one I'd ever had. My body shook as I cried out. I thought it was going to last forever. It was so intense it left me breathless and weak. Once Buzz withdrew, my legs crumpled, and I lay on the ground panting.

Buzz laughed and then lay down beside me. His hand caressed my stomach, sending shivers up my arms.

"What was that about?" he asked.

"I don't know. I just wanted a fuck," I replied. I didn't want him to know I was turned on by the orgy.

"And I'm happy to oblige, but something must have set you off. I've never known you to be so demanding."

"There's a lot you don't know about me," I smiled. "I guess it's all the good looking men around me. I got turned on."

"And now? Are you satisfied or can I do more to help with the itch between your legs?"

I wasn't about to argue.

It was around four o'clock when we got back to the others. Too exhausted to party, we rolled out our sleeping bags and climbed in.

Most of the Wolves continued their revelry, some didn't sleep at all. I fell asleep listening to the sound of rock music and quiet murmurs. I woke up alone, to the same sound.

I found Buzz standing with a couple of the officers by a table surrounded with an assortment of guns. I knew they were associated with guns but to see so many lined up was a shock. Buzz noticed me watching and discreetly indicated for me to walk away.

More business was conducted throughout the day. Bikers, old friends and new acquaintances rode up and were welcomed into our camp. Cars pulled up while the occupants went off with one or two Wolves to discuss business. Buzz asked me to be a hostess to our guests. I was happy to associate myself with the Wolves, the more I could participate, the more I was welcomed.

Word soon got out about where we were camping. By late afternoon, there were more unassociated bikers present than the Wolves. As long as they gave us the respect we deserved, they were more than welcome. Business was business after all.

I made the mistake of announcing that I was going into town to buy some cigarettes. The next moment, Wolves were asking me to pick up their own smoking supplies. I left the camp with a list, three pages long. Thankfully Rig and his Lady Jewels, had the car and were in charge of the beer stock, so carrying the cigarettes and Rizla supplies on my bike wouldn't be a problem.

Matlock was breathtaking. The shopping forgotten, I parked my bike and then walked along the picturesque lakes and bridges. The town was small, clean, and quaint; with village stores, tiny cafes, and Matlock's famous fish and chip bar.

The Wolves weren't the only bikers in Matlock. Everywhere I looked, black leather was on show. Most of the bikes looked as though they'd just come straight from the show room. Chrome polished, until you could see your reflection; lights, clean and sparkling. Some of the bikes' artistic paintwork put Clay's work to shame. My pride and joy was a heap of junk compared to these rides.

I noticed a couple of Wolves sitting outside a small pub. Because I wasn't one of them yet, I had no right to go over and strike up a conversation, so I headed back to my bike.

I'd just stepped out of the shop, arms loaded with bags, when two young guys stopped me.

"Are you rolling with those bikers camped outside Matlock?" one asked.

"The Wolves, yeah I know them. What are you after?"

A few seconds passed before one answered.

"We were hoping you could hook us up. We're having a party this weekend, and we're looking for some party favours."

I knew what they were after. Even though I didn't have the authority to make any deals using the Wolves' name, an opportunity to bring something into the club had come up, and I wasn't about to let it pass.

"Follow me," I said.

We walked around the back of the shop. I wanted somewhere less public.

"Take your shirts off," I ordered.

They looked at one another, shrugged, and then un-buttoned their Hawaiian style shirts. The last thing I needed was to be played by police. Once they were bare-chested, I told them to drop their trousers. They did without hesitation.

I walked around the back of them and checked for wires.

"Okay, get dressed. What are you after?"

"Some Whizz," one answered, as he pulled up his trousers.

"And some Ice, if you have it," the other one added.

"Not a problem," I lied.

I didn't have a clue what they'd just asked for. But I'd seen enough drugs around the camp to know the Wolves probably had whatever it was the guys wanted.

"How large is this party?"

They looked at one another again.

"10 rocks and 20 grams of Whizz should do it."

Again, naive like I was, I had no idea if that was a lot. I decided to push it further.

"Hell, no. We don't deal less than 20 rocks and 50 grams of Whizz."

They walked away, huddled together and whispered. I was kicking myself. I thought I'd blown the deal. Seconds passed, and then they came back over.

"It's a lot more than we need, but I reckon we can shift it. How much?"

Now this I couldn't wing. I didn't know what the street price was.

"Hey chill. You'll get a good deal. You got transport?"

"Yeah."

"Good. Follow me."

I rode back to the campsite with the guys following in their car. My heart was pounding. I was worried I'd made a big mistake. I had no association with the Wolves. Would Buzz be pissed at me for taking the initiative?

I pulled my bike over to the side of the road. The camp was just ahead. The car pulled along side me.

"Wait here," I instructed, and then took off.

I found Buzz, pulled him to one side, and told him about the deal.

"What does your gut tell you?" he asked.

"It's kosher, I checked them out. Just two guys wanting to score some supplies for a party."

"Okay, tell Jive what you've just told me. Tell him to sell the Ice for 30 large, and the Whizz 17 a gram. Stay with him while the deal's made."

I turned, as he called out.

"Hey, Dior, that was a good sale."

I walked away smiling. I'd just brought something into the club; I hoped it was enough to get patched.

I figured Buzz had upped the street price, thinking the guys were suckers. Jive's black greased, shaggy hair and muscled biceps gave him the appearance of someone you shouldn't try to barter with. I hoped this might encourage the customers to go with the offered price.

The guys weren't going for it and moaned that the

price was too high, until Jive offered to throw in a free gram of Special K.

The deal made, the customers walk away happy with their score and the Wolf pocketed nearly £2000.

"What's Special K," I asked Jive, as we walked back to his bike.

"Here," he said, taking out a blister of tablets and giving me a white pill.

I knew I should have kept my mouth shut, but I wanted to learn about the drugs I was dealing, and what better way than to experience the effects myself. I put the pill in my mouth and swallowed it.

Jive grinned. "You're okay, Dior," he said.

The pill quickly took effect. I felt alive, like the world was different and everything around me; the trees, people, voices, were all new to me. I felt energetic, as though I could do anything.

The money I made for Buzz kept him on a high without the use of drugs. However, my behaviour didn't go unnoticed.

I couldn't give him a straight answer. Most of what came out of my mouth was gibberish.

He left to find Jive.

I found out the next day that Special K had the same effects of PCP. That I'd heard of, and I'd sworn I'd never touch the stuff. Yes I dabbled, but I wanted control. I wanted to enjoy the experience but still be lucid. I didn't want to be so fucked up on acid, I didn't know what I was doing or thinking.

What made matters worse, Jive had accidentally, (so he said) given me a 200mg dose rather than a 100mg. It wasn't long until the hallucinations started.

Apparently, Buzz went mental at Jive when he found out what I'd taken. Moving me away from the camp, he ordered the Wolf to keep an eye on me.

I don't remember much of the experience. Jive told me what happened.

He said I was screaming about killer squirrels, and then I got up and started dancing around while trying to catch rainbows. He told me that nothing I said made any sense and at one point I freaked out so bad, he ran and got Buzz. Buzz made me swallow a Temazepam tranquilizer, hoping it would bring me down. He stayed with me for the next ten minutes until the pill started working and I calmed. I guess I was coming around, because I recollect feeling drowsy and wanting to sleep, but Jive continued talking to me. I remember wishing he would just shut the hell up.

I woke up late the following morning, feeling weak, and it took a while before I managed to sit up. Jive was propped up against a tree. His eyes were closed. I noticed his left check was swollen and bruised. I wondered if there'd been a fight in the camp. My head was throbbing and I had a terrible thirst.

He woke up and looked my way.

"Hey, Dior. You're awake. You okay?"

"Yeah," I answered, rubbing my temples. "What happened?"

"I'm real sorry. I fucked up, gave you the wrong pill. You had a bummer trip. Buzz had me down here all night watching you."

"Sorry you missed the party," I mumbled.

"Hey, it's not your fault. I shouldn't have given you anything in the first place. He wasn't impressed," he said, rubbing his swollen check. "You ready to roll?"

"Yeah, man."

Jive laughed.

Buzz was chatting to a small group when we rode up. The others were packing up their gear and loading their bikes. It was time to go home.

Jive disappeared as Buzz strolled over.

"Jem's going to ride your bike back. You'll be with me. It's not safe for you to ride."

"Okay," I said. I couldn't agree with him more, there was no way I had the strength to hold the bike up, let alone ride for hours.

"How you doing?"

"I've got a major headache and no energy, apart from that, I'm fine. I don't remember much."

"Man! I could have killed that shit when I found out what he'd given you."

"I could have said no," I argued.

"Listen, Dior. I don't want you taking any more Amphetamines. It will fuck you up. Stick to blow, okay?"

"Yeah, sure," I answered, surprised that he worried about my well-being.

"I'm gonna round up the pack, and then we're leaving. It wasn't a great run for you was it?"

"What I remember of it was great. I've learned a lot," I answered.

CHAPTER NINE

My mobile rang shrilly, waking me up. It was Sunday morning and I'd planned to have a lie in, especially as I didn't get in until four that morning.

"Hey, Dior, it's Sly."

I rubbed the sleep out of my eyes.

"Yeah," I answered.

"I want you to deliver something to a friend of mine. I promised him I'll be there by ten, but Buzz just phoned and wants to see me."

It didn't sound like a request. I remembered Buzz telling me I'd have to do whatever the Wolves asked.

"Yeah, okay. I'll be there in a bit."

I got dressed and left without breakfast.

Sly was standing outside his house, waiting. The place looked large enough for four bedrooms; I wondered if he had any kids. He handed me a small parcel no bigger than a paperback book, and then gave me a piece of paper with an address written on it.

"You know where it is?" he asked.

"Yeah, sure."

There were no thanks. No goodbye. Sly went back inside and shut the front door.

Putting the parcel inside my jacket, I climbed onto my bike then rode down to the address he'd given me.

The friend lived in a block of flats a short distance from Sly's house. It didn't look like a bad neighbourhood, so I wasn't too bothered about parking my bike outside. I walked up the flights of stairs and was happy to see the staircase clean. Potted plants stood in the corner at the top of the stairway. The residence I was looking for faced the top of the 2nd floor. There wasn't a door bell, so I rapped on the glass panelled, wooden door.

The middle-aged guy who answered was barefooted and dressed in jeans. With short black hair, and thick black rimmed glasses, he didn't look to me like a biker.

"Sly asked me to drop something off for you," I said.

He looked me up and down and then smiled. "Very nice." Opening the door, he gestured for me to go inside.

I hesitated, not sure if walking into the guy's apartment was a wise thing to do.

"Well, get in. I'm not doing this outside." Stepping out of the house, he looked both ways before grabbing my arm and ushering me inside.

Once the door had closed, I handed him the package.

He walked over to the dining table, placed centrally in a small, but tidy living room, and hastily opened the parcel. An assortment of pills separated in small plastic bags, and a large bag of what looked like weed fell onto the table.

"Good," he said, as his hand shuffled through the produce. "Tell Sly I'll settle up with him on Tuesday and ask him to hook me up with some snow."

"Will do," I answered, and turned to leave.

"What's your name," he called.

"Dior."

"You Sly's Lady?"

"No, I'm with Buzz."

His attitude suddenly changed.

"Really, pleased to meet you, Dior." He shook my hand "Thanks for this, you're a life saver. He's a sound guy, your ole man."

"Yeah, and don't you forget it." I said. Cliché, but I was feeling powerful.

I left him to his score, and walked out of the flat with a big smile on my face.

My mobile rang just as I was pulling up into Clay's drive. Caller's ID told me it was Buzz.

"Morning," I answered, cheerfully.

"Where are you?" He barked.

"Just got home. I'm about to jump in the shower. Wanna join me?" I sniggered.

"I'm at my place, come down."

"What? Now?"

"Yes. Now!" The phone closed.

It wasn't a nice invitation; I realised something was up.

I walked into his house and found him in the kitchen. Newspapers covered the table, while parts of oily machinery sat on top.

"Hey. What's up?" I asked.

"You made a delivery for Sly?" he asked, without looking at me.

"Yeah, he told me to drop something off at his friend's."

"Did you know it was drugs?"

"No," I lied. "Not until the guy opened the package. I thought you knew about it. Sly said you'd called and that he had to wait for you and couldn't make the delivery."

"Did he now."

Buzz threw the greased rag he was holding into the sink.

"You're so fucking gullible," he spat.

I stared at him, hurt by his insult.

"What I mean is you're naive to this lifestyle. Your innocence is going to get you into trouble. Sly's known as a dealer by the cops, they've probably got him tagged. That's why he told you to make the drop. Didn't it occur to you what would happen if you'd gotten caught?"

I'd been too busy following what I thought were orders, to worry about the serious implications of what I was doing.

"You need to wise up, Dior," he continued. "From now on, you don't take any orders, unless they come from me, okay?"

I nodded my head "Okay. Sorry, I honestly thought you were cool with it."

"I've got people who take the risk; you're not one of them. I'll deal with Sly later. Come here."

I went to his open embrace, not caring he was going to get his oily fingers all over my white top.

"You're a baby. Everything's new to you, but you've got to get tough, and I don't mean physically."

"I'm trying," I said, and nuzzled my head into his chest. "You want a drink?"

"I wouldn't say no to a cold coke, and roll me a joint while you're there."

I did what he asked, and then sat at the kitchen table watching him cleaning his cycle parts.

"I agree. I'm an innocent when it comes to this lifestyle, but I'm learning, and I want to learn. Will you teach me?"

"Sure," he said, taking the joint from me.

That evening, I found out that Cocaine was known by thirteen other names including, Coke, Dust, Snow, Toot, and Crack. Cannabis, which I already knew as Dope, Blow, Grass, and Weed, was also known on the street as Draw, Black, Bush, and Ganja. Barbiturates, which Clay and Beth had given me, were known as Pink Ladies, Sleepers, Nemies and Blue Devils. Buzz told me they were hard to come by, but were easy to sell. I already knew Ice was another name for Methamphetamine, and the street name for Speed was Sulph and Whizz. He told me about weight, the street price for each drug, and the effects.

Now I knew, I didn't need to experiment anymore.

I'd only smoked dope since he told me to lay off the other stuff. I was cool with that. The dope gave me the fix and high I needed. Buzz dabbled in everything at regular intervals. But he wasn't hooked and I'd never seen him with a needle or track marks on his arm. Yes, I was looking. I'd heard too many horror stories about heavy drug use. I didn't want Buzz turning into a junkie.

I also found out that evening that Tray kept a bag of Rohypnol, the date rape drug, behind the bar for when it was needed. I wondered how many bags of those tablets they went through each month.

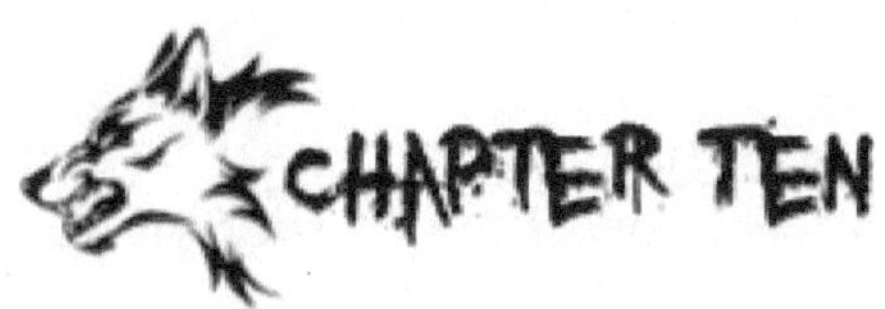

CHAPTER TEN

On Saturday, we went on a run down to Yarmouth, just the East chapter of the Wolves. We wanted to ride, chill, and party with our brothers.

If we were going to travel any further than that, I would have been on the back of Buzz's bike. But I loved the freedom of riding my V Rod, and being part of the convoy of bikers was thrilling. We were given respect on the road. No one tried over taking, it would have been impossible anyhow; because of the length of road we took. We took our time and no one dared to complain.

We'd just hit the road again after a stop off at a pub. I was riding last, behind the patches and Lady Wolves.

I had no idea where we were going, so when they turned into a disused quarry, I followed.

Trent had the sudden urge to go scrambling on his Honda Shadow. I looked around the quarry and saw the heaps of sand he was stupidly thinking about riding over and jumping. The quarry was a fenced off work site where they were tunneling into the side of the mountain. Unfortunately, that day someone forgot to lock the gate.

I watched and laughed, as around ten Wolves started riding around the quarry, shouting encouragement to one another as they played motocross on their Harleys, Yamahas, and Hondas. Saber then challenged Buzz to a race through the unfinished tunnel.

"You up for it, Dior?" He asked.

"Hell, yeah," I answered. Any opportunity to impress the guys.

Buzz, Saber, Trent, Rig, and I sat at the entrance of the tunnel and opened the throttles on our bikes.

I soon got the feeling we'd made a serious mistake. As well as racing one another, we had to dodge rubble that had been left around. Rig was in the lead, I was second. Trent, Saber, and Buzz weren't far behind.

No one saw the metal sheeting in front, until it was too late.

Spread across the width of the tunnel, the sheet was standing upright; right in the paths of our speeding bikes.

Rig ploughed straight into it. The front wheel of his Yamaha Roadster hit the metal and flipped the bike, throwing him over the sheet. Less than a second later, the bike followed.

I quickly swerved, missed the metal, and crashed into the side of the tunnel wall instead. My bike rebounded and smashed into Saber's Kawasaki. I saw another bike go down, but didn't know if it was Trent's or Buzz's. It all happened in a matter of seconds, and I will never forget the horrific sound of the screeching brakes and crushed metal.

I was alert but couldn't move, and the pain in my shoulder and chest was excruciating. I found it hard to breathe. I wanted to get up. I couldn't lie there and do nothing, while the others needed help.

I soon heard the loud roar of motorbikes coming up the tunnel. I guessed the noise of the crash had alerted the rest of the Wolves.

"Fuck, call an ambulance," someone yelled.

There was too much noise, and I tried to close my ears to it. The pain was so intense I thought I was going to black out. I closed my eyes and then opened them again when I felt someone lifting and holding my neck.

"What the fuck are you doing? You're not a fucking Doctor? Don't touch her," I heard Buzz yell.

Buzz knelt beside me. He was out of breath and panting. I couldn't believe he was okay. I wanted to reach out to him, but I couldn't move. The paralysis scared the shit out of me.

Ten or more bikers were standing around looking down at me. I wanted to get up and let them know I was fine, but all I could do was allow the tears to run down my face.

"Okay, take it easy," Buzz said gently.

I tried to nod but the intense pain in my neck and shoulder made me cry even more. I closed my eyes and wished the spectators away.

"Help's on its way. Lay still," Buzz said.

As he moved away, I wanted to call out, beg him to stay with me, but I knew the others needed him.

Karen soon took his place. Holding my hand, she talked gently.

I felt cold and started shivering. Someone laid a jacket over me, and I closed my eyes and allowed the pain to take me away.

I was the lucky one; I left the hospital with only a broken collarbone. Rig was dead before the ambulance arrived. His bike had landed on top of him and crushed his chest. Buzz told me death would have been instant, and that he wouldn't have suffered.

Saber's leg was crushed when my bike bounced off the wall and slammed into him. Trent's was the other bike to go down. He braked sharply and then slid off his bike, breaking his elbow in the process. Buzz braked and managed to control his bike. He saw the whole thing and replayed each moment to me.

Under Buzz's order, half of the chapter carried on down to Yarmouth. The rest of the Wolves hung around the hospital.

Buzz wouldn't leave my side.

The Wolves never caused trouble or cheeked the nurses; it was their sheer number that put the fear into the staff. In the end, the doctors discharged Trent and I just so they could get rid of the rest of them. Saber had to stay in for surgery on his leg; Elf remained and made sure the damaged bikes made it back to London.

I was surprised we were still going to go down to Yarmouth after what happened, but Buzz was adamant we had something to celebrate.

There was a party atmosphere when we arrived at the camp. They treated Trent and me with honour, carefully carrying us through a procession of chanting bikers.

I had survived my first serious bike crash, and in the Wolves' eyes, that made me a true biker.

I asked Trent why the bikers weren't mourning Rig.

"This is mourning," he told me, handing me a beer. "We're celebrating his life. He was a bad-ass biker, and he rode hard. He lived and died the lifestyle. He had a biker's death. I can only hope to go the same way."

I agreed with what he said. What better way to go. Dying, doing what you love with the thing you loved the most. Bikers lived for their bikes, and they died with them; it was the only way they wanted to go.

We extended the trip for an extra day. I was high most of the time, doped up on Codeine. It turned out to be a great run considering.

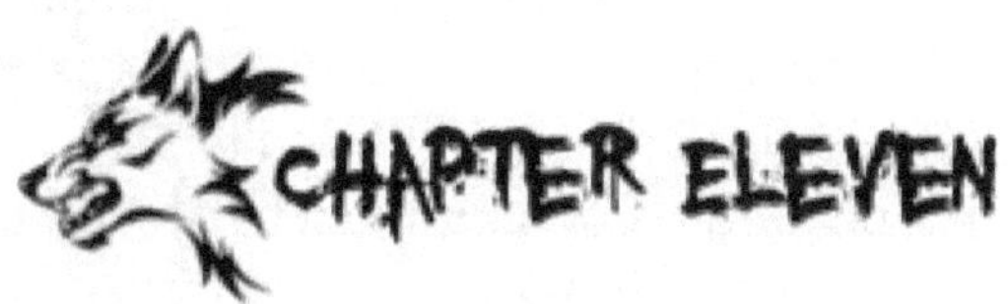

CHAPTER ELEVEN

It took a nearly a month to recover from my injury. And it had been far too long since I last visited Beth and Clay.

"Hey, long time no see." Clay greeted me at the door with a hug.

"Yeah, sorry. I've been busy," I smiled.

We walked into the house. I put my helmet down on the kitchen table, and then gave Beth a hug.

"You look good," she commented.

"Thanks, I'm doing well."

"How are you settling in your new place?" she asked.

"Fine. I still haven't finished unpacking yet, though," I lied.

It had been nearly two weeks since I'd been back to my own pad. I lived at Buzz's and I didn't use my place much. Most of my clothes were at his apartment.

"So, what you been up to?" Clay asked, as he offered me a rolled joint.

"Been gigging most nights and then spend my day working on articles." I hated lying to them, and hoped they wouldn't see through me. "How's work?" I asked him.

"Busy." He replied, gazing intently at me.

"What?"

"I don't know - you seem different."

"Nah," I said, nudging him with my shoulder, "I ain't changed. Home grown?" I asked, passing the joint to Beth.

"Of course," she smiled.

I didn't like the way Clay was trying to read me.

"You staying for dinner?" he asked, his eyes still straining to see something that wasn't there.

I knew I needed to be careful what I said and how I acted around him. He was a smart guy.

"Sure. Umm - talking about dinner. What you guys doing next Friday evening?"

"Got nothing planned why?" Clay asked, as he exhaled the smoke.

"I thought it was time I invited you both for dinner, at my place."

"You cook?" Beth laughed.

"Hey, I have to look after myself now. I clean, wash, and cook thank you very much. You'll see," I grinned. "So, Friday at eight, yeah?"

"Sounds great," Clay said, with a tight smile.

I knew the only way I would be able to get through the afternoon without causing any more suspicion to Beth and Clay was if I was stoned. So I did just that. They didn't mention about my intake or my refusal to accept any pills. Once I relaxed and dropped my guard, I was back to my usual quirky self.

***

When I told Buzz I wouldn't be back that Friday night, he never questioned me. He'd never taken me for granted.

Once Clay and Beth knew where I was living, I couldn't risk him finding out, in case one of them came around unexpectedly. Buzz knew I had my own place, but as we were comfortable living at his, he never once mentioned about staying over at mine.

Living the lie was killing me. I was lying to my family, my friends, my lover, and myself. It was tearing me apart. And I knew it couldn't go on.

I took my rucksack, which was stuffed with notebooks and paper, out of the bedroom cupboard where it was hidden. It was a ritual I did every two days. Not wanting Buzz to suddenly come back to the apartment and catch me working on some article, I did most of my research and write ups at the library. I had a hard time concentrating though. I would be sitting at one of the wooden desks with my laptop open, and I'd suddenly get the feeling I was being watched. I know it was just paranoia, caused by me trying to hide my vocation. But I always thought, what if Buzz did have someone following me; what would happen if the Wolves learned they had a journalist in their camp?

When Buzz asked me what I did for a living, I told him I was a home helper; going around pensioners' houses, cleaning, shopping, and doing daily chores. He didn't question me any further. I'd deliberately chosen something that would be boring to discuss. Plus, there was no way he could pick me up after work because I never had a regular station.

Having a nine to five job stopped me from getting to know the Wolves better. Buzz didn't work, and I didn't like having to sit behind my desk when I could have been with him. If I wanted to get inside the motorcycle club, something would have to give.

***

I brought some magazines, old newspapers, and left them lying in various positions around the living room. Sneaking my toiletries out of Buzz's apartment,

I filled my bathroom with them. Towels hung on the rails and my closet was filled with clothes I no longer wore. The apartment had to look as though I was living there. Turning the stereo on, I got to work in the kitchen. I was going all out for Beth and Clay; stuffed mushrooms with feta cheese, chicken in red wine sauce and cheesecake for dessert. I was a good cook and Buzz had never complained about my culinary skills.

The apartment soon filled with the aroma of baked chicken and mushrooms.

Clay and Beth turned up at the apartment just after eight. The table was set, the food ready. I double checked the apartment to make sure everything looked in order, and then opened the door to them with a smile.

Neither of them had made an effort to dress up, not that I expected them to. Both turned up dressed in jeans and T-shirts. I was wearing black trousers and a green, silk, wrap shirt. My hair was pinned up, and the heat from the kitchen had curled fallen wisps of hair.

I wanted the evening to be fun, but I felt uncomfortable at first, like I was sitting opposite strangers. Conversation was stilted. The drink and dope came out, and we began to loosen up. Once Clay relaxed, he had a lot to say and left Beth and I in hysterics.

When desert was over, we took our drinks and sat down on my pink, soft, couch. I was feeling mellow by then. There were a few minutes of silence and then Clay turned to me with a serious expression etched on his face.

"I thought you'd talk to me if something was bugging you," he said.

"What you talking about?" I took a deep drag of my joint, held it in for a few seconds, and then blew out the smoke. My head was spinning.

"You know we're good listeners; we won't judge," Beth added.

"I know you better than anyone," Clay continued, "Probably better than you know yourself. I never beat about the bush."

I stared at him.

"We know there's something going on with you. We're not stupid. No matter how hard you try to hide it. I'm pissed that you won't confide in me."

He looked hurt.

Any other time he would be the first I would talk to. But how could they understand? I was hanging with the Wolves; seeing the son whose father murdered Dylan.

"Can't get one across you can I?" I smiled weakly.

Both looked at me with expectancy.

"Yeah, there's something going on. Something that's ripping me apart and when I'm ready to talk about it, you'll be the first to know—" Clay was about to interrupt, but I held my hand up and continued. "I'm confused and I have to get this shit sorted in my head before I can talk about it."

I thought they'd drop the subject. No such luck. Clay kept on.

"Is it something to do with Jade and Marcus? You know you can talk to us about them. We wouldn't keep anything from you."

I shook my head.

"Then John? I understand what you're going through. It's not easy to lose someone close. I miss him a lot as well."

My eyes started to well up.

"No. It's nothing like that. Just leave it okay?"

Clay was silent for about five seconds. "Then work, if someone's bothering you…"

"Clay! Drop it. I don't want to fucking talk about it." I stood up and left the room.

I heard Beth and Clay arguing.

I know it would have been easier to continue denying that anything was wrong, but Clay was no fool. I didn't want to have to avoid them. I loved them as though they were family, and sometimes you need normality in your life.

When I returned, the mood had lightened. We spent the rest of the evening joking and laughing with one another. The argument forgotten, we chilled out with cannabis and rock music. They didn't leave until after one AM. I thought about going over to Buzz's, but I was too stoned to ride anywhere.

***

The following evening, Buzz took me down to the club house. We found the place full; most of the East chapter was present. I thought maybe there was a party, someone's birthday. We chatted, greeted our friends, and then sat with Trent and Sly at the bar. Ten minutes had passed when Karen and Jem came over and asked me to come outside with them. I didn't get the impression there was a problem, so I jumped off my stool and followed them through the back exit.

They stood in front of me with attitude. Karen stood with her hands on her hips and glared at me. I wasn't scared, just surprised. I wondered what I'd done to set them off. Karen could be a mean bitch; I'd seen her fight and didn't particularly want to take her on.

"Take your jacket off," she ordered.

"Why?" I asked. My stomach tightened.

I didn't want to fight her or Jem, I thought they were my friends, but something was bugging them. Nevertheless, I was ready.

Wolves came storming out of the club house and circled around the three of us. They were waiting for a show down. I was more concerned about what I was supposed to have done, than worried about the pending fight.

"I said, take your jacket off," Karen said, in a calm but warning tone.

I looked to Buzz and he nodded. I took off my jacket and handed it to Karen.

"Come on then," I said, standing in a fighting stance with my fists out.

Karen smirked. Jem laughed.

"We just want to sew on your Lady patch you silly bitch."

Before I had time to react, the Wolves ran at me and showered me with beer, shaking the can then pouring the froth over my head, with yells and hollers of delight. I was dripping wet, and screaming. I'd thought I'd drown in foam. I stood there shivering, soaked from head to toe, while the Wolves surrounded me, with congratulations and welcomes into the club. The Ladies patted me on the arm, some dared to embrace me, not caring they'd get wet doing it.

I'd made it. I was a member of the Wolves. It was one of the proudest moments of my life.

Buzz stood on the sidelines watching me with a huge grin on his face. He followed Trent and the others back inside, while I squeezed the beer from my hair and sodden clothes.

A Lady named Jugs—perfect nick-name for someone with a 38 double-D bust—handed me a towel and informed me there were dry clothes waiting for me in the office.

"Thanks," I grinned, and then followed her inside; dripping wet, my feet squelching in my shoes.

After I'd dried and dressed, but still stinking of beer, I rejoined the Wolves. I wanted to buy my brothers and sisters a drink to celebrate, but as the club house had an open bar, I suggested we continue the party down at the Drunken Squid. They accepted my invite with cheers and howling.

As I sat on the back of Buzz's bike, proudly displaying the white, Lady title, I'd never felt more proud.

It was one of the best nights of my life. I forgot why I was there, about the Tyrants, about what the Wolves represented. That night I was surrounded by love and respect given freely by my brothers and sisters; my new family. That night, I felt I was home.

Although Buzz was attentive, he wasn't openly affectionate. I was his Lady, I was a Wolf, and there was no need to advertise the fact.

We celebrated when we got home. Although I was so drunk by then, I don't remember how long our private celebration lasted. I woke up naked, lying beside him. My head was throbbing and I felt sick, but as I lay there watching him sleep, looking at the gorgeous, fit man lying naked beside me. I thought I'd burst with contentment.

CHAPTER TWELVE

Almost one fight kicked off every week in the Drunken Squid. Most of the time it was just between two bikers. However, if Buzz deemed it necessary, a Wolf or two would jump in and help their brother.

The pub was crowded for a Tuesday evening. I heard that the group of bikers in the bar was on a run down from Northampton. They seemed friendly enough and gave the Wolves the respect they demanded, until an argument kicked off between Big Al and one of the bikers. From the sound of raised voices, it looked as though things were going to get rough, and I wondered if there was going to be a bar-fight.

Big Al's opponent didn't stand much of a chance, outdone by size and talent. The biker could have taken a punch or two and walked away minus a couple of teeth. However, when Big Al suggested they take it outside, the biker stupidly agreed.

I asked Buzz what had started the argument. He shrugged his reply.

Maybe he had something to prove, maybe standing

up to a Wolf would earn him respect. However, the rest of his group stepped away. They had no intention of backing up their friend, or starting with the Wolves. They stood on the sidelines and watched their friend get battered.

Big Al swung his huge fist and almost knocked the guy out with one punch. The biker staggered, shook his head, and then ran at the Wolf, intending to head butt him in the stomach. With one hand, Big Al swatted him away. The Wolves laughed and cheered.

I couldn't work out whether Big Al taking off his jacket was a good or bad thing. The Wolves reacted to the action with gasps and cheers. Buzz leaned toward me and answered my question.

"Make sure you don't take your colours off when you're fighting," he warned

"Why?"

"We want those who see the fight to know it's a Wolf that's kicking the shit out of the other guy. The patch identifies you. You take your colours off once, and you get a warning, twice, and you get the patch etched into your back."

I gasped. "You mean someone actually gets a knife and cuts the image into the back? Surely you wouldn't do that to a female?"

Buzz shrugged. "It hasn't happened yet, but it could."

I cringed at the thought of someone sketching into my back with a blade.

"I'm guessing Big Al had his first warning?"

"Yep." Buzz smiled.

"Shit!"

I watched Big Al throwing his punches and wondered if he realised what was going to happen to him after the fight.

"Don't let it bother you." Buzz smiled. "The ones that have had it done use any opportunity to strip off and display their war scar. Elf deliberately took his jacket off twice during fights just so he could get the tattoo."

"What about you? Would you do it?"

He gave me a lopsided grin. "Do I look fucking stupid?"

Big Al stood in front of the biker and beckoned him to get up. Once the biker was on his feet, Big Al smiled and gestured for him to throw a punch. It was the only time his fist connected with Big Al's face, but it didn't have an impact.

The Wolf smirked. The biker went down quickly.

Big Al walked back into the pub amidst a chorus of cheers.

"When's this punishment supposed to happen?" I asked.

"Now. They'll take him back to the clubhouse and do it there. You don't want to miss it."

I was grossly curious to see it, and to see how many Wolves it would take to hold Big Al down. If it was going to happen anyway, I might as well watch.

The Wolves piled out of the pub ten minutes later, started their bikes, and rode down to the clubhouse.

Shade was the tattoo artist called upon to mark the big bad Wolf.

I cringed and turned away as the knife cut, etching the infamous head of a Wolf into his skin. Blood ran from the wound and soaked the paper that lay beneath him. Four Wolves held his legs and arms. Nevertheless, Big Al was a large man who took the pain with naught but a grimace. I assumed he was so doped up, he couldn't feel anything, but Buzz said they didn't allow the biker any pain relief. It was a punishment after all.

I learnt a good lesson that night. Never to take my jacket off in a fight, no matter how hot I was.

***

I didn't want to walk straight in, but then again, I felt I shouldn't have to knock, so I did both. Tapping softly on the door before opening it, I then walked down into the cellar of the Drunken Squid.

The guys were sitting huddled in the far corner, away from the crates and barrels.

I saw the guns laid out on the table, before one of them covered them up with a tablecloth.

Buzz turned his head sharply around.

"What is it, Dior," he asked.

I could tell from his tone that he wasn't angry with me for interrupting their discussion.

"A couple of Warlocks have just walked in the bar."

"Only two?"

"Yeah,"

"Introduce yourself. Be nice to them and then invite them here for a chat," he said, and turned back around.

"Okay." I walked back up the stairs wondering what kind of business the Wolves wanted with the Warlocks.

The two bikers were sitting at the bar drinking their beer. I walked up to them, ready to play the hostess.

"Hi, I'm Dior," I said, and smiled.

They introduced themselves as Clive and Abs.

"You know Buzz?" I asked.

"Never heard of him," one answered.

"He's the president of the Wolves. This is our bar."

"Hey, sorry, we didn't know. Look, we don't want any trouble." They rose from their seats.

"It's cool. The Wolves don't have a problem with the Warlocks. You're welcome."

I called the bar man over. "Tray, get these gentlemen another pint. It's on me," I told the bikers.

"That's mighty kind of you, ma'am," one said, and raised his glass.

Whether it was because they had heard of the Wolves, or because they knew they were in an MC's territory, they showed me respect. I was in awe of the Warlocks, their reputation, and the patch they wore. Their accent told me they weren't from the UK; probably American or Canadian.

"Listen. When you're done, Buzz would like to meet you."

"Sure," one answered.

I waited until they had only a small amount of beer left in their glass, and then invited them down into the cellar. It wasn't a great place to conduct business, but at least it was private. An old sofa and a small coffee table had been placed in the left corner, giving the cellar a more homely feel. I was surprised not to see a TV or fridge. They had a telephone though, and air conditioning for the hot summer months, a small heater for the winter. Neither was on that evening.

I stayed while introductions were made, and then Buzz sent me back upstairs for beer.

When I returned, everyone seemed to have loosened up. Laughter and a cannabis fog filled the cellar.

"Dior," Buzz called. "Is that blonde in tonight?"

He was referring to a young girl who had started hanging around the bar; another that had fallen for the bad-boy image. Lucky for her, she never tried to hit on Buzz. She seemed happy to be part of the lifestyle and just to hang around with the Wolves.

"Yeah, she's here, bothering Jazz," I answered.

"Bring her down; we could do with some entertainment," Trent said."

The bikers sniggered.

I walked back up the stairs and into the bar. Two things were bothering me. The first, I knew exactly what entertainment Trent was referring to; there was going to be a gang bang and the Warlocks were invited guests.

I couldn't bring myself to take her downstairs without warning her first. The second thing, was the likelihood that Buzz was going to have a go, after all he was the president and had to set an example. I couldn't stop him, but it hurt to think he would dip his rod, especially now that I was his Lady. I wondered if he would walk away and leave the others to it. I doubted it.

"Hey, come here," I said to the blonde. Then grabbing her arm, I led her to the other side of the room.

She was thin, tall and looked young; too young. Wearing a mini-skirt, which left little to the imagination and a small white and black T-shirt, her outfit was certainly attention-seeking. The long, black, suede boots she was wearing added to her height. She was pretty and that just made me more anxious for her.

"What's your name?"

She looked nervous; I would have been in the same situation.

"Cassie," she answered.

"Look, Cassie. The Wolves want you downstairs, there's a party of seven, and they're looking for action. Take this," I said, and handed her a Rohypnol.

She shook her head. I expected her to be scared and want to run, but instead, her eyes and face lit up.

"Are they fit?" She asked me.

I wanted to slap the fucking slut. She knew what was going to happen if she went down, and yet she wanted it. She was going to be fucked every which way by seven large bikers, and she was looking forward to it. I just couldn't get my head around it. Did being part of the lifestyle mean that much to her?

I had no choice. I'd been drugged and didn't know what was happening. However, I gave her the choice. Maybe she didn't realize that once they had her down there and things started getting rough, no amount of pleading and screaming would make them stop until they'd had their fill.

She was a slag and deserved everything coming to

her, I thought, as I walked back down the stairs to the cellar with Cassie following close behind.

Buzz had gone out of his way to impress his guests. An assortment of drugs covered the table and lines of coke were cut and ready.

"You want a hit, ma'am?" The fattest of the Warlocks asked me. His beer belly hung grossly over his jeans.

I smiled at him and shook my head. "No thanks. That shit will fuck up my voice, and I'm a professional singer, so I can't risk it. Thanks all the same."

The biker poised the rolled up note over the powder and then snorted. Sniffing, he rubbed his nose a couple of times, then lay back into the chair.

"You want some?" Trent asked Cassie.

"Yeah, sure," she answered.

I knew the stupid bitch had never touched the stuff before and was trying to impress the bikers.

As she leaned over the table to snort, Trent put his hand up her skirt. She parted her legs and groaned.

I'd seen enough.

"Enjoy yourself guys," I said, and then leaned down and snogged Buzz. I was marking my territory, and he knew that.

I was still sitting in the bar when the bikers came back up. There were handshakes, pats on the back, and then the Warlocks walked to the door. They nodded to me before leaving, and I waved them a goodbye.

"When the skank wakes up, put her in a cab." Buzz shouted across to Tray.

"So, did you fuck her?" I asked, as I wrapped my arms around his neck.

"Why would she interest me when I've got you?" he answered.

We kissed, and I tasted her on his lips.

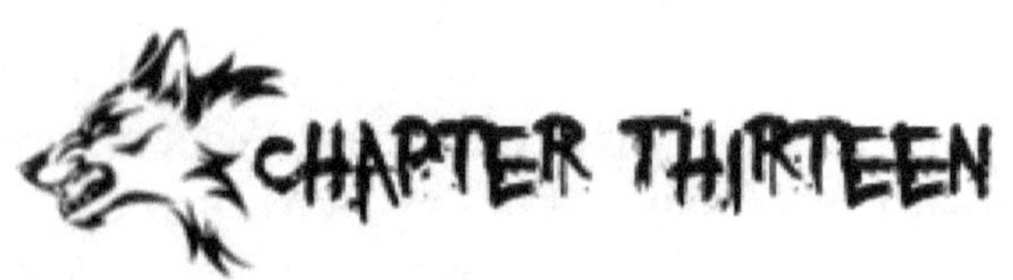

"I went to see my dad the other day." Buzz said causally, as we were reading the newspaper.

I had the entertainment page, and he was reading classified; always on the look out for cheap cycles and parts.

"He's getting an early release. He'll be out next month," he continued.

I looked at him, but didn't know how to feel; scared, happy? Finally, I was going to come face to face with Dylan's killer. I needed to get my head and my shit together and figure out how I was going to kill the bastard. I'd gotten side-tracked. Buzz and the Wolves had taken over my life and my thoughts. I was too comfortable. I forgot why I was there.

"How do you feel about that?" I asked him, hoping for an idea of how I should be feeling about this sudden news.

"Once he's back, he'll take over the presidency, and I'll have more time to spend with you."

He held me in a tight embrace.

"I told him about you, and he's looking forward to meeting you."

As I am, I thought.

He pulled away and then reached over and grabbed his beer from the coffee table. "Umm. How are the auditions going? Have you found another band to sing with yet?"

I shrugged. "Nah, I don't feel good singing with anyone else. It's not the same; I miss Todd and the others."

"Maybe it's for the best," he said, passing me a spliff.

"What do you mean?" I asked, lighting the joint and inhaling deeply.

"It's just…"

"What, Buzz? What is it?"

"A few of the Wolves are musicians and Mud thinks it's a good idea for you to start something up with them."

"You've got to be joking?" I spluttered.

"No. He's serious. Actually, what he said was, he doesn't want you singing in bars. You're a Wolf, and he reckons a rock singer is below a Wolf."

"What the fuck!" I said, and stood up. With my hands on my hips I stared at Buzz waiting for the punch line.

"Hey, they're not my words. He wants you and the band to play at the clubhouse for his welcome home party." He grinned.

"You find this funny?" I asked. My stomach was beginning to knot.

"Nah, it's my dad, assuming he's gonna be thrown a welcome home party. That's just typical of the conceited shit. I suppose I'll have to arrange something. And you'll have to set something up with the guys."

Knowing how he felt about his dad calmed my anger.

"I could do it as a one off. But I'm looking for a band to play with, Buzz. You know how much I love performing." I sat back down beside him and took the joint from his fingers. "And I can make good money from singing," I continued.

I know," he said. "But Mud doesn't want you socializing outside of the club, until he gets to know you."

"No one tells me how to run my life. I'm not fucking waiting for his permission. I haven't even met this man, and I already hate him."

"Get in the queue." He smiled tightly. "How do you think I feel? I've had to put up with his shit and his orders since I was a kid. When Mum dumped me on him, I was thrown into this lifestyle, not by choice, but it's all I've ever known. I warned you babe. Once you're a Wolf, you become their property, and Mud's gonna make sure he works you." Taking the joint from me, he took a deep drag, held it in, and then continued. "It's best if you start rehearsals right away. The guys will probably need some practice."

"Are they any good?" I asked.

"No."

"Well, this is fucking great. I'm forced to sing in a band of amateur musicians, with maybe two performances a year; every time a fucking Wolf is let out of jail."

Buzz laughed. I rested my head on his chest.

"Hey, you'll be paid for it," he said.

Man, I was as mad hell. I hadn't been singing, but I always knew I could have. It would have been a way for me to separate myself from the Wolves and feel like an independent person. But now Mud, the fucker, had taken that way from me. But that's why he did it. He didn't want any of the Wolves to have a normal life. If I quit my fulltime position on the paper, the Wolves would own me. Any other time, I would have told Buzz and his father to go fuck themselves, but I was so close. Too close to walk away. For the time being, I had to grin and bear it.

***

To say that these guys needed practice was an understatement. Pug, named so because of his ugly face, thought he could play the drums. He was great at making a noise. Although I wasn't a drummer, I was the one teaching him which beat to play for each song. Saber was the most talented. I already knew about his love for playing the guitar, but he was nothing like Todd. At least he could play, and he learnt fast. CK was our bass guitarist. Unfortunately, when we got together, he only knew three chords. Saber and I soon changed that.

One thing I can say about the guys, they were dedicated. Thrilled at having the chance to play in a band, and with me as the lead singer, they gained confidence quickly. They didn't want to fuck up and make a fool of themselves in front of the other Wolves, so they practiced hard, listened to what I had to say, and learnt all the new songs. Of course, they had their own idea of what they wanted to play. I gave in and allowed each of them to perform their favourite rock song. Mostly, we stuck to the songs ChainMail had played. CK came up with the name Death and Destruction, which I turned down. The name didn't seem important, especially as we wouldn't be playing gigs. I decided on Road Rage. I think the guys liked it, but didn't have much say in the final decision. I was the boss after all.

Pug got a new set of drums, and money didn't seem to be a problem when it came to supplying the band with instruments and equipment. Buzz was forever surprising me. Was there no one this guy didn't know?

Within two weeks, we were actually sounding like a rock band. We had one week left until Mud's home coming party. I knew the guys would be ready in time. They weren't about to embarrass themselves or me.

# CHAPTER FOURTEEN

The Sheffield run was my first as a patched member, and up until Saturday evening, it had been great fun; loads of laughter, drinking, getting stoned, messing with one another's head. A couple of scuffles broke out between members, but it was harmless, playful fun. It was great to be able to join in with the discussions and not be told to take a walk. People acted like they wanted to hear what I had to say.

Nothing can compare with camping under the stars with a fit bloke wrapped around you, the freedom to be myself and not be judged. It was being part of a bikers' run, hanging with your family, which made people want to live the lifestyle. The freedom was addictive.

Getting drunk in our camp wasn't enough for the Wolves. They wanted their presence felt. We left a small group behind to guard camp, and then headed into town in search for a decent pub. I wasn't sure, and I never asked, but I wondered if Sheffield was known as a bikers' town. There were an awful lot of bikes parked outside fast foods and pubs.

Buzz signaled, and pulled over to the side of the main strip. Plenty of leathers were on show, bikers walking around and hanging outside the bars. Another twenty five bikes followed suit, we took up most of the left side of the road, parking our rides in between other bikes. Our arrival caused a stir, but we relished the attention our colours brought. We were obviously the largest motorcycle club on show.

Buzz now had a thing about the Wolves' rides looking good before a run. Anyone turning up with a dirty cycle was banned from participating, and fined. Our bikes were a talking point.

There were some bikers sitting on wooden benches outside a pub called the Green Street. They were watching us but we ignored them and filed inside. The pub was a lot larger than it looked from the outside, but with thirty plus Wolves and the customer already inside, the place soon became busy. This caused more bikers to come inside and see what the deal was. We weren't there to cause trouble; we were just chilling, having a drink and a chat with other bikers and toughs.

Elf came running up to Trent and yelled. "Some fucker's just slashed your tyres."

We rushed out of the bar and climbed back on our bikes. I threw my keys to Trent then jumped on the back of Buzz's ride. Elf headed the group, and we followed, waiting for him to point out the biker who messed with us.

It wasn't one, there were five of them, and they were running hard, their black jackets billowing behind them.

They picked the wrong route, I thought, as Buzz sped up. The rural road was wide and muddy, which slowed down the runners. Large, wired fencing blocked off any escape route except straight ahead. We gave chase and it was exhilarating, the cool wind blowing through my hair, the speed. I wanted more. Turning my head, I looked past the Wolves' bikes, and saw another seven bikes following us. I guessed they wanted to see the show. I never thought about what would happen when we caught up with them. How serious the beating would be. I, like the rest of the Wolves, was enjoying the chase.

Elf overtook one of the guys and spun his Suzuki Bandit around, blocking the biker's escape. Jumping off his bike and on top of the man, he quickly had him pinned to the ground and was throwing punch after punch. Three other bikes stopped. The rest of us kept up with the hunt. The four guys had reached the end of the road and split up. Trent stayed on Buzz's tail.

I wanted us to catch the guy who slashed Trent's tyres. No one messes with a Wolf. I was curious to see what would happen.

One of them got away; the other three got a hospitalized beating, even though they denied any wrongdoing.

It was late by the time we got back to camp. The Wolves who stayed on guard were pissed that they missed the chase.

We were sitting around the campfire playing out the beating again, when three motorbikes came roaring up.

Buzz and Trent stood up and walked over to the bikers. Jive and King quickly followed. Karen turned to look at me. I guess she smelt the tension as well. The air was thick with it.

Buzz hurried back over to the rest of us.

"They've found him. He's a member of the Omegas. They're in their clubhouse. Leave everything. Let's hunt."

The Wolves leapt up, hollering and whistling as they ran to their bikes and suited up. Everyone was caught up in the electrifying atmosphere. There was going to be a clash. We were ready. We wanted it.

We followed the bikes down to the Omegas' club house, and then the three bikers took off. Buzz didn't shout out any instruction, it was as though they'd done it a million times before. We were walking into Omegas' territory, without a second thought. The Wolves looked ready to kill. They jumped off their bikes. Holding chains, sticks, and knuckle dusters, they stormed the club.

By the time I got inside, the fight was well underway. Two of the female Omegas had Jugs cornered and were beating her bad. I jumped on top of one of them and started punching.

The Omegas were good fighters, but the element of surprise gave us the edge. The Lady Wolves had just as much to prove as the men, and we were relentless with our assault. I knocked a woman out and then stopped to catch my breath as I looked around at the chaos. A few of the Omegas were on the floor, some groaning, others unconscious. I saw a Wolf laid out, but I didn't know who it was. Buzz was fighting a guy the same size as himself. A couple more punches and the bikers were going down, I thought.

What I saw next is etched in my memory for the rest of my life.

Big Al and Elf were holding a biker in restraints. Big Al had his arm around the guy's throat and Elf, who stood behind, had hold of both of the biker's arms. The man had to be the one who had slashed Trent's tyres, I thought, as Trent was standing in front of the biker yelling at him. A blade was in his hand. I watched as Trent slashed the guy from the top of his chest, down to his stomach. Two clean strokes as though he was drawing and X.

They let the biker drop to the floor and then repeatedly kicked the guy as he lay in a pool of dark blood. The powerful odour of blood, smelling of iron and copper metal, made me want to vomit. There was so much splattered on the floor, the furniture, and the walls. It looked like a scene from a horror film.

My head was throbbing after being whacked with something. My knuckles were swollen and sore, and I didn't think I'd have the strength to punch again. The Ladies were finishing off the female Omegas, and I kicked a couple of male bikers who were too injured to fight back. I'll never forget the sound of grunts, glass smashing, screams, and boots crunching bones.

"Enough," Buzz shouted.

I turned to see his left eye was cut, blood dripping down his face. I watched him limp out of the bar. Jive was out cold and had to be carried out. Karen had a black eye and a bloodied lip. Most of the Wolves were pretty banged up, but we left the club house elated. We'd done what we came to do. Proved a point, and left a message. No one messes with the Wolves! We left the Omegas lying injured and bleeding on the floor of their club house.

Although we needed to rest, it was too risky to stay at the camp in case the cops showed up, or another MC wanted a bash at the Wolves. We were in no fit shape for another clash and that made us an easy target. Tired and weak, we returned to camp, packed up our gear, got back on our bikes, and hit the road. We were riding for another fifteen minutes, when Buzz found a wrecking yard. Riding around the back, I saw the cars stacked up high, giving us the privacy we needed.

I took care of my man, who I was surprised to see came away from the clash with only a bruised face and damage to his right hand, although I wondered how he managed to ride his bike with the injury. After I'd finished cleaning him up, he took care of me. I flinched, as he wiped antiseptic across my bloodied lip. He made me soak my hands in warm, salty water and then looked at my head.

"You'll live," he grinned.

We looked at each other and smiled. Although there were moans and groans from injured Wolves, spirits in the camp were high, and soon we were laughing and joking again.

In the morning, we packed up and headed into town to fix Trent's bike. Sly moaned about his busted hand and the fact that Jem was riding his bike back to London. Partnered with Saber, the Wolves teased Sly, calling him a Bitch.

The town was quiet; most of the bikers had gone. Trent's bike was still in one piece, and we were surprised it hadn't been taken apart. I assumed news about the clash got around and no one dared to mess with his bike.

We hung outside the pub and watched the guys work. We looked like we'd been on a pile up. Scratch that, we looked like we'd been in a violent clash, maybe that's why the public stayed out of our way. Our bruises and cuts didn't go unnoticed by the residents. Our hardened appearance made them even more wary.

I secretly hoped we wouldn't be going on another run for a few months. I imagined it would take a very long while to get over the incident and forget the smell of all the blood.

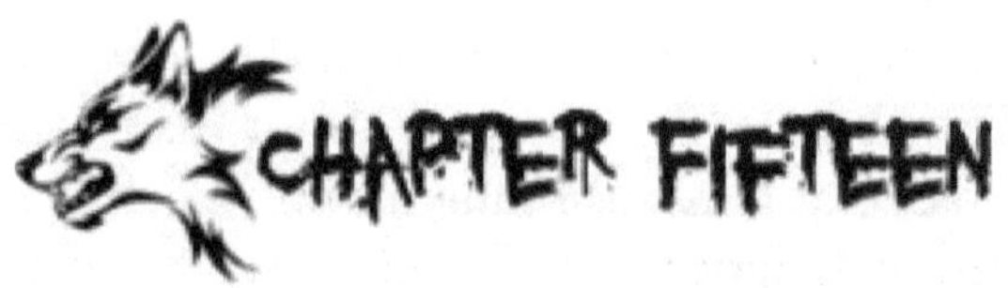

CHAPTER FIFTEEN

I could have done without performing that night. I was nervous about meeting Mud, without having to put on a show for him as well. It was enough to make me feign an illness.

We'd been performing for ten minutes, and I was half way through singing "Bat Out of Hell" when Buzz and Mud walked into the club house. Claps and cheers erupted as the Wolves rushed over to greet their president. They gave him a hero's welcome, and it sickened me.

The band stopped playing and jumped off the stage to add their welcome. I retreated around the back. My heart was pounding and I needed a strong joint.

I didn't know what to expect, certainly not the biker who had been picked up by ten Wolves and paraded around the club amidst cheers and chants of his name. The guy was big; at least two hundred pounds. Both of his fat, muscled, arms were inked out. With a shaven head and orange-painted beard, he gave the appearance of a bad motherfucker, someone you would likely see behind the bars of a maximum security prison. He nodded and smiled to his brothers, but left me with the impression that he rarely laughed. His attitude was tough and serious; totally out of my league.

Slicing his throat was the only real damage I could do with my knife. And even then, I couldn't see my small blade having any deadly effect. And how the fuck was I supposed to walk out of their club house after killing their president? My hands shook. I knew I wouldn't be able to find the courage to even attempt to kill him. He'd probably break my wrist before I had a chance to attack.

The dope was helping me relax, but not enough. I couldn't get the image of Mud out of my head. He looked nothing like Buzz, which made me question whether Mud was Buzz's father.

The laughter and cheering continued until Saber came into the back and informed me it was time to go back on stage.

We started with "Heart 16". I kept my eyes on Buzz and the other Wolves, but when my sight happened to fall onto Mud, he'd be looking at me through almost black eyes, as though he was seeing something others couldn't see, and that unnerved me.

I finished the first half and left for the back room. I needed another smoke. No. What I needed was an Amphetamine.

The guys continued playing, displaying their not so talented skills, and allowing other Wolves to jump on stage and Jam. I sat chilling with my smoke, while listening to a biker screaming out "Born to Be Wild" down the mike.

Buzz showed up, sat with me, and shared the rest of the joint.

"What up?" I asked. He was unusually quiet, which worried me.

"Mud wants to meet you."

"Now?"

"Yeah, he's in the office."

I sensed Mud didn't like me. I couldn't decide whether it was because he didn't think I was good enough for Buzz, or because I was too good. Whatever, the feeling was mutual.

My heart was racing, and my stomach knotted. I was scared. I'd been waiting for this moment, to be alone with Dylan's killer and get revenge. The thought made me shiver, but then I remembered it wasn't just Dylan I was avenging. He might not have murdered my brother, but in my opinion, he sure as hell was the cause of John's suicide. I was a Wolf's Lady and patched member, but I was thinking about murdering in the forgotten name of the Tyrants.

I did consider how Buzz would react, though. He'd never forgive me and would probably lead the hunt. And although I loved him, I needed to remember why I was there, after everything the bastards had put me through; vengeance was keeping me sane.

My knife was in my jacket pocket, and as I didn't want to face Mud without my colours and certainly not without my blade, I took my jacket off the hook, put it on and then followed Buzz to the office.

As we neared the office door, Buzz leaned in close. "Do whatever he says," he whispered.

I stared back at him. I understood what he was implying. This wasn't going to just an introduction. Mud wanted a piece of me, just like the rest of the Wolves.

"He won't hurt you." Buzz promised.

His assurance did nothing to ease my anxiety. I put my left hand into my jacket pocket and held on tightly to my knife. Taking a deep breath, I walked inside.

Mud was sitting behind his desk scanning through

club accounts. He looked up as I entered. Clasping his fingers, he leant back in his chair and gazed at me. I wasn't about to lie about how great it was to finally meet him. I wasn't sure if I should step forward and introduce myself. Mud spoke first.

"I've been hearing a lot about you, Dior. It seems you've been a busy Lady."

I smiled.

"I like a woman who takes the initiative. You've certainly done your share in the time you've been with us. Why is that?"

I hooked a finger from my other hand, on the waist of my trousers and shrugged. "I want to prove I'm a valuable member of the Wolves. I'm sure others will tell you that."

He nodded his head. "Yes, like I say, you've come up in conversation. But you've been trying too hard, and that worries me. You're a smart, talented woman. What do you want with the Wolves?"

"I met Buzz. I fell in love with him and the lifestyle. There's not much more to tell. I just want to fit in."

He got up, walked around the desk, and stood in front of me.

"I'll give you the benefit of the doubt, but I'll be keeping a close eye on you. Buzz told me his feelings. It won't last long. He'll get bored and soon find someone else to fuck around with. He always does. He's gone through more skanks than anyone. Take your jacket off," he ordered.

I couldn't ignore his instruction, and I didn't have the opportunity to take the knife and hide it somewhere else. I had no choice but to take my hand out of my pocket and discard my jacket.

He ran his finger down my neck and along the outline of my breast. I didn't flinch. I didn't say anything.

"Oh, yeah, I've heard all about you," he breathed hard against my check. His breath stank of stale beer.

"It's been a long time since I've touched a woman."

I glared at him.

"Don't worry, I promised Buzz I wasn't going to fuck you. But now, looking at you, I don't see why I shouldn't."

He laughed, and then pulled me to him. Pulling my corset down, he groped and sucked my breasts, and then nibbled at my neck. I felt relieved that his actions did nothing for me.

"You're going to show me just how talented that pretty mouth of yours is."

It would have been the perfect moment to slash the bastard's throat, but my knife remained in the pocket of my jacket, thrown some distance away. I didn't like the idea of having to go down on him, but I knew I'd gotten off lightly thanks to Buzz.

"Very talented," he sniggered, as he got dressed.

I wanted to run out of the office, put my fingers down my throat, and get rid of every bit of him.

He walked back around the desk, sat down, and glared at me.

"My son's a fucking idiot," he spat. "He's allowed this corporation to fall. He ain't got a fucking clue how to run a business. But I'm back now and things are gonna change. You'll soon get to see who the Wolves are, and then we'll see how long you stick around. Go on, piss off; there'll be a riot if you don't get your pretty arse back on stage."

I picked up my jacket and then turned to leave.

"Tell Gina and Jugs to get in here," he called.

I nodded, and then walked out of the office and relayed his message. The women immediately left to satisfy their president.

I leaned over the bar and ordered a coke. I needed something sweet tasting. I felt an arm go around my shoulder and turned my head to see Buzz standing beside me, with a look of concern.

"You okay?" he asked.

I nodded and then turned my head. I couldn't look at him. I couldn't talk to him. So many emotions were flooding my mind and spirit. I needed to sort out my head, but first I had to get back on stage and finish the set.

I don't know how I got through the rest of the evening. I forgot the words to "Fire and Ice" and fucked up the chorus of "Look but Don't Touch". I refused to listen to their chants of an encore, made my apologies, and left the stage. I didn't see Mud leave the office and imagined what was happening inside. I wondered if Jugs and Gina enjoyed it, whether they were turned on by him.

He referred to the Wolves as business, a corporation. They weren't just bikers. They weren't his brothers. He was using them, plain and simple. Mud intended to increase the business, and I had a feeling that would include more than just guns and drugs. Suddenly, killing the bastard wasn't my only option. I had to stop him, but murder wasn't my only weapon. I was a journalist. My job was to investigate and report.

# CHAPTER SIXTEEN

"I'm sorry, James, either I work in a freelance capacity, or I'll have to stop working for you altogether. I have too much on; I don't have time to be on the clock anymore. I spend more of my time outside of the office than I do here. So what's the difference?" I told my editor.

"The difference is I know where you are. Freelance writers charge more than permanent staff, and you work for me," he moaned.

Once I made up my mind to investigate the Wolves illegal activities, I knew I wouldn't be able to continue full time at the paper.

"Hey, I'll still be working for you; I just get to pick and choose when, and what I want to work on. I'll go easy on my rates, and I'll even let you set the deadlines, so you can feel like my boss."

He scowled.

"I'll tell you what. What if I make sure I'm in the office for a couple of hours every two days? That way, I can type up any finished work, give you the pieces personally, and chat about my next assignments."

He looked doubtful and shook his head. "I need someone full time, Sofi. If you can't do the job, I'll have to find someone else."

I called his bluff. "Fine, if that's what you want. I'll just have to find another paper to freelance for. You know there's plenty that will gladly take me on. I may just contact *The Eye*."

I knew that by mentioning our competitor's name, James would think twice.

"Now, just a minute…" he paused. "Maybe we can come to some sort of arrangement."

"That's the spirit," I grinned. "I'm loyal to you, James, don't think otherwise. I'm head-hunted every month, but I've never wanted to leave here. I just don't have the time for a permanent position anymore."

"Okay, I'll see what can be done."

"Thanks, you're a star," I leaned over and kissed him on the cheek. He turned red.

"I'll call you in a couple of days, when I've got myself sorted, and we can talk about my rates."

"Yes, yes," he said, and ushered me out of the office.

*****

I was standing by the bar in the Drunken Squid chatting with Saber, when Suzie, a hang-around, came up to me.

"Mud wants me to go down on you," she said.

"You what!"

"He said I have to go down on you."

"You dirty bitch, get the fuck away from me," I yelled, and shoved her. I was not and would not run that way, and I was no exhibitionist.

"It'll be fun. I'm sure you'll enjoy it," she said.

I took a step toward her, my hand clenched in a fist. "You come near me again, you skank, and I'll fuck you up alright."

Mud's laughter drowned out the rest of the Wolves' sniggers. I glared at him, and he smirked.

Buzz was out of town, up West in a meeting. I decided that if I hung around the Drunken Squid I might hear something to incriminate the Wolves.

I turned my back on Mud and continued my discussion with Elf.

I don't remember the rest of that night.

Buzz shook me awake. It was early morning and the sun was coming through the curtains.

"Hey. What time did you get in?" I yawned.

"Around two. You were sleeping. I didn't want to wake you. Dior, did you take anything last night?"

"No." I answered, and sat up in bed, surprised by his question. "I promised you I wouldn't unless you said it was okay. Why?"

"Cause I had a hard time waking you up. But now that you are, why don't you show how much you missed me."

I didn't need asking twice.

He didn't leave the house again until late afternoon. I stayed home to make a roast for dinner, while Buzz took a ride down to the pub.

He came back twenty minutes later. The door slammed shut and he rushed at me. I backed up against the wall. It had been a while since I'd seen him angry.

"What's wrong?" I asked.

"Had a good time last night did you?" he spat. "Oh, yeah, I heard all about it."

"About what? What are you talking about?" I touched his arm.

He recoiled, and pushed me against the wall.

I couldn't understand why he was so angry. What was I supposed to have done?

"You and Suzie put on quite a show last night. I heard everyone got off watching."

"That's bullshit," I yelled. "The skank come on to me, said Mud wanted her to go down on me in front of the whole pub. I told her to get the fuck away from me and warned her what would happen if she didn't."

"So, you don't remember anything happening?" he asked, in a calmer tone.

"No. Buzz, nothing happened. Hell, you should know me better. Do you really think I'd participate in something like that? I'm a performer of songs not some fucking porno star."

He gently caressed my cheek.

"I'm sorry, Dior. I just hate it when someone trashes your name. If I find out who spread this rumour I'll fucking kill them. The thought of you lying there, with your…"

I put my finger to his lips and stopped him from saying any more.

After a tense dinner, we took a ride down to the Drunken Squid. I'd hardly been in the place for five minutes when Buzz came storming up, grabbed my arm, and started dragging me to the door.

"What's going on," I cried. Thinking I was going to get smacked around. His temper scared me.

Outside, he let go of my arm and took my hand as he walked hurriedly toward his bike.

I knew from his gesture that he wasn't angry with me. But I wished he would tell me what had upset him and why we were leaving in such a hurry. I thought that maybe we were going for a ride, so he could cool down, but then I recognized the road. We were heading to the clubhouse.

He braked and skidded to a halt. We got off the bike, and then he grabbed my hand, and with his other, pushed the club door open so hard, it slammed against the inside wall.

"Where's Mud," he barked at the group of bikers who were playing pool.

"In the office," one answered.

"Wait here," Buzz said to me, and then marched to the other side of the room.

I watched him storm into the office, the door slammed shut.

Saber came over.

"I guess he's heard about Mud slipping you a rope last night. Tray locked up and it was one big orgy."

I turned my face away. I felt sick. Yet again, I'd been drugged and forced to humiliate myself in public. I understood why Buzz was so mad.

The bikers in the room had become silent, as we all stood and listened to the muffled yelling coming from inside the room.

The expression on the Wolves' faces told me that this was a serious argument.

"I've never seen Buzz act this way about any other woman. What the fuck have you done to him?" Big Al asked.

Suddenly there was a crash and the sound of moving furniture coming from the office. The Wolves hurried over, yanked open the door to the office, and rushed in to try to separate Mud and Buzz, who looked as though they wanted to tear each other apart. Buzz fought the two bikers who attempted to restrain him.

"Get him the hell out of here," Mud yelled. Spitting blood on to the floor, he then wiped his mouth with his arm.

The bikers started to drag Buzz out of the room. I stood beside the open door, watching.

"I've had enough of you fucking up my life," Buzz yelled. "Stay the hell away from me and Dior. And if you ever pull another stunt like that, I'll fucking kill you."

Once out of the clubhouse, the bikers let go of Buzz.

"Hey, cool it man," Big Al said.

"Fuck you." Buzz yelled. "And fuck the Wolves."

If any other person other than the vice president had said that, they would have found a knife in their belly. Big Al stepped forward but I pulled Buzz away before anything could start.

We got back on his bike and rode home.

I thought Buzz would have calmed down by the time we got back to the apartment, but his anger was still boiling. He slammed the door shut and tore his jacket off in disgust. Anything breakable was thrown on the floor. I watched, not sure whether to approach him or not. Nevertheless, I thought I knew how to make him relax. Walking over to him, I grabbed his waist. My hand reached down, but he flinched.

"Don't. I'm not in the mood," he said.

"Sure." I shrugged, but was surprised; it was the first time he'd said no to any sexual relaxation. "Do you want to talk about it?"

"No."

But he did. We sat together on the couch and shared a joint while he talked about the hate for his dad.

"The guy just pushes me the wrong way. Always testing me to see how far I'm willing to go in the Wolves' name. No more. I'm not taking any more of his fucking orders."

"Can't you just walk away?" I asked.

"No—yeah, I don't know. Things are different now. Since I've met you, the Wolves don't seem important. I can't stop thinking about you. I want to spend my time with you, not stuck in the clubhouse or Drunken Squid with a group of outlaws. What the fuck have you done to me?" he grinned, and then leant forward with his head in his hands.

"So, you don't want to be a Wolf anymore?" I needed to know. Just the idea that he might walk away, left my heart thumping.

He sighed and leaned back into the couch. "That's easier said than done. I don't know any other way to live, Dior. It's who I am."

He looked so sad. I pulled him to me.

"You're wrong. That's not who you are. These last few months I've been seeing this amazing man. He's loving, kind, has respect for me, and I can imagine spending the rest of my life with him."

"You serious?" he asked, sitting up and staring at me.

I nodded.

"Shit, Dior. If it was so easy, we'd pack up and leave together, right now."

I wanted to ask him why not. Why couldn't we do that? But I kept silent. I'd heard enough. He gave me what I needed. If the opportunity came, I knew we would pack and leave together.

"What was it like growing up with the Wolves?"

He paused before replying. "Each day I was looked after by one of my dad's women. There were always bikers around the house, drugs and drink. I think I was eight when I tried my first magic mushroom. I was never alone, but I never had kids my age to play with. I suppose it was exciting in a way, but like I said, I didn't know any better." His eyes glazed over while his memory re-played. "I was around ten when I realised the Wolves were outlaw bikers. We were on a run down to Skegness. I wasn't allowed to go on many of the runs—and I was glad—because I was ignored and ended up spending the weekends on my own while Mud and the rest of them got high. But on the Skegness run, another group of bikers turned up at the camp. There was a clash, and I saw things that a ten year old boy should never see. I lost respect for the Wolves and any love I had for my father. I didn't realize what he was capable of."

He became silent again.

"What changed?" I asked. "Why didn't you carry the hatred with you?"

"I keep replaying the moment in my head. I'll never forget that day—I was sixteen, walking home from school on my own when I was jumped by four guys. The attack was planned, payback for something my dad had done. What better way to get retaliation than to kick the shit out of the president's son? They beat me up bad. I remember lying there, wishing I was dead. I thought I was dying. It shook me up and it was a while before I dared to show my face on the street again. Mud told me if I wanted to survive in this life, I had to get tough. And so I did. I never allowed another person to touch me. I became tough, bitter, and violent. I became a Wolf. Once I put the jacket on, Mud owned me. I did whatever he asked and had no qualms about doing it."

"And now?" I needed to hear him say the words.

He smiled. "And now I have you. You bring out the nice guy in me, and I prefer living that way. Let's not talk about this anymore. How about going to see a movie?"

"Haven't you got a club meeting tonight?" I asked.

"Fuck it! Let's get dressed up, leave the colours at home and go out and party."

"You serious?" I said, jumping off the couch.

"Hell, yeah. You're my Lady. It's about time I treated you like one. You've got an hour. Go on, get ready." He laughed.

That night, we forgot about the Wolves. Buzz left his tough, public image behind in the apartment along with his colours. Dressed in black trousers and a cream shirt, he was a handsome date; attentive, romantic, and loving. We walked hand in hand around the town, then went to the cinema and watched a romantic comedy and afterwards went for a Chinese. It felt as though we were a normal couple and had been dating forever. We laughed, talked non-stop about anything and everything, embraced and kissed at every opportunity. It was a side to Buzz I'd never seen. The kind of guy every girl dreams of meeting, and he was all mine. I knew things would be different in the morning, but for now, I was living a dream and enjoying every second. He was polite, and even apologized to someone when they bumped into him. If he were wearing his colours, the guy would have been on the ground.

CHAPTER SEVENTEEN

I decided that the morning hours were the best time for me to snoop around the clubhouse office. Nicking the keys from Buzz, I rode down to the clubhouse and let myself in. The windows were blacked with black paint, so even though it was daylight outside, it was almost pitch-black inside. I knew my way around the clubhouse well enough to get to the office without bumping into anything.

I didn't want to take photos of the evidence, I wanted paper proof. The first file I pulled down from the shelf held a record of all the patched members names and addresses, monthly account of paid dues, expenses, and incoming revenue. Unfortunately, it didn't list where the revenue came from, but I knew in time I'd find out.

It was a huge risk, but I had to take the page and photocopy it, as there wasn't a copier in the office. Luckily, the pages were in a ring binder, so I didn't have to take the whole folder with me. Rolling the page up, I put it in the inside pocket of my jacket. I'd just put the folder back on the shelf when the office door opened.

I immediately dropped to the floor. But not quick enough.

"Dior?"

Still crouched on the floor, I looked up and saw King staring down at me.

"King, what you doing here?" I said, and moved so I was kneeling comfortably.

"I could ask the same thing of you," he answered.

"You haven't seen a gold hoop earring around have you?" I asked, while leaning over and running my hand along the beige, corded carpet. "I lost it last night." I turned my head around to catch King, staring at my arse. I smiled. "You know how it is, passion takes hold, and things get heated. I've got to find the fucker, it cost me a fortune."

To my surprise, King got down and on the floor and started searching around. After a couple of minutes, I sat on the floor feigning defeat.

"It's probably underneath one of those bloody cabinets," I said, slamming my hands on my knees in frustration. I got up on my feet. "Oh, well. You win some you lose some. Come on, I could do with a drink." I linked my arm with his, and we left the office and sat at the bar for a drink, chatting about motorbikes and rock music.

I didn't know King as well as the others. I knew he was a club officer, but I didn't know what he did for the club. His muscular build made up for his short height. I'd never seen him without a Union Jack bandanna on his head. I wondered how many of them he had, or did he always wear the same one? I guessed his head was shaven, but with bushy brown eyebrows, I imagined what he would look like with long hair.

King had the oldest cycle in the chapter. A Norton, it was a collector's item and his pride and joy, but the bike had a hard job making a long run. Many times, we'd have to pull over while he fixed or tightened something on his machine. Buzz teased him, calling King's ride a piece of junk. I'd love to know what he really thought of my V Rod.

King never questioned me about how I got into the clubhouse. He must have assumed I got the keys from Buzz, which in a way I did.

Everything worked out. I got the keys back before Buzz noticed. That evening, I made sure we had sex in the office. After I put on my underwear, then lay on the couch, I asked Buzz to get me a drink.

The moment he left the office, I jumped up, grabbed the page from my jacket and managed to get it back into the folder and put the folder back on the shelf before he came back.

I felt exhausted. I wished there was an easier way of gathering the evidence. I sighed.

Buzz took it as a sign that I was ready for round two.

We only left the office when Mud came storming in and told us to clear out.

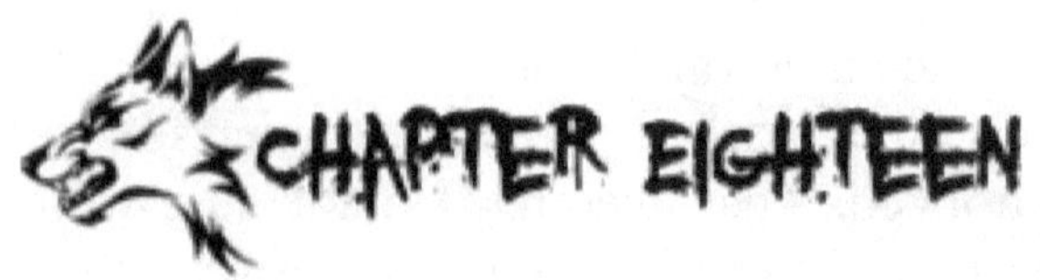

CHAPTER EIGHTEEN

The Wolves were willing to sacrifice their lives for one another. It wasn't just a line. And I was a Wolf.

It was a Saturday evening. Half of the chapter was down at the Drunken Squid; a few of them had gone to see a band down at the Two Thorns. Since I'd stopped gigging, I didn't enjoying watching other bands perform. The rest of us were at the clubhouse, smoking pot, playing pool, and just chilling. Mud was shut up in the office; I wondered what he was doing, but smiled at the thought that on Sunday morning. I'd snoop around and find out.

A group of motorbikes pulled up outside. Jive looked to see who'd arrived.

"It's the Hawks," he yelled.

Buzz jumped down from the bar stool and rushed outside along with five other Wolves.

I grabbed Jem's arm. "Friend or foe?" I asked.

"They've a tough rep, but not from around here. We've never had problems before."

"What do you think they want?"

"Who knows? Come on, let's find out."

We ran outside to see six Hawks standing in front of the Wolves, giving attitude. They looked tough enough. Their appearance was no different from our club. All bikers dressed similarly. The jeans, tattoos, and leather were their signature.

Buzz was having a heated argument with one of the bikers, and then swung a punch, flooring the guy. I stood on the steps with Jem and watched the fight. Blocking the Hawk's punches, Buzz thumped the biker in the gut and face. The Hawks were hard. They knew how to fight, and as both groups were equal in numbers, I knew it could go either way.

"You'd better get Mud," I said to Jem. She ran back inside.

Buzz's eye was cut open and blood was dripping down his face, Jive got a knuckle duster in his face and was on the ground being kicked. Two of the Hawks were on the ground while Saber and Sly stamped on their faces.

I don't know what caught my eye, but as I turned my head towards a bush to my right, I saw the barrel of a rifle pointed at Buzz's back.

No," I screamed, and ran forward.

A crack rebounded around the car park. Buzz turned around and I stumbled into him.

Mud ran outside. "Get that son of a bitch," he yelled.

Four of the Wolves gave chase, while the rest of the Hawks crawled over to their bikes. Mud let them go.

"You okay?" he asked Buzz.

"It's Dior, she's been shot."

His words didn't make sense to me until I looked down. A small red dot just under my left collar bone was pumping out blood at an alarming rate. My knees gave way and I collapsed onto Buzz. He pulled me down to the floor, screaming for an ambulance.

"No," I yelled. "No hospital." My voice sounded weird. I wasn't sure if they heard me. So I yelled again.

"Okay, okay, babe. No hospital." Buzz said, looking alarmed.

"Oh, shit," I said, looking down at the blood that had dyed my skin. My pink corset was now wet and stained dark.

Buzz reached up and took the towel someone was holding out, and then pressed it to the bullet wound. Until that moment, I only felt a dull throb, but the moment he applied pressure, the pain racked through my body and I cried out.

"I'll call Med," Mud suggested, taking out his mobile. I guess he didn't want a corpse on the Wolves' doorstep.

I couldn't see well. Images were blurred around the edges. I shivered, and then wondered why I was feeling cold, as sweat was running down my face. I tried to lift my arm to wipe it away, but I couldn't move.

"Dior, hold on babe, please," Buzz begged.

I tried to focus on his face. His lips were moving but I couldn't hear what he was saying.

"Buzz," I called.

He bent his head down.

"I love you," I whispered, before my eyes closed and my mind went to another place.

I opened my eyes and found myself in what looked like a doctor's surgery. I was lying on a hard, black, trolley bed. The walls were painted white; a large, dark, wooden desk sat in the corner of the room.

Buzz was sitting on a chair, bent over, with his hands on his head. I tried to sit up, but it felt like a huge weight was pushing down on me. I had an IV attached to my right hand, my left shoulder was bandaged, and my arm wrapped in a sling.

Buzz leant back in the chair, with a deep sigh; he stretched, ruffled his hair, and then turned toward me.

He'd been crying. His face was wet and his eyes looked red and tired. A smile spread across his face when he saw me.

He rushed over. "How you feeling?" He asked, as he caressed my hair.

"I've been better," I joked.

My voice sounded weird; hoarse and weak. My mouth was so dry my tongue was sticking to the roof of my mouth.

"Can I have some water?" I asked.

"Nil by mouth," a rough voice answered. The Doctor came out of another room adjoining the surgery.

I looked up at the large man in the white coat. Black wispy hair hung down onto his round face, his fringe was long but the rest of his hair was cut short. He had kind blue eyes that twinkled when he smiled.

The doctor checked my pulse and blood pressure and then shone a torch in my eyes.

"What's your name?"

"Sof... Dior," I said, almost given my real name.

He smiled. "Do you know what happened?"

"Yeah, I took a bullet saving this guy's life," I answered.

Buzz squeezed my hand.

"Yeah, you saved my man's life," the doctor answered, patting Buzz on the back. "I removed the bullet and you're going to be alright. You lost a lot of blood, and you're gonna be weak and feel pain, but we'll do all we can to make you comfortable. Ten minutes and then you have to leave," he said to Buzz. "She needs rest." He squeezed Buzz's shoulder before going back into the other room.

I leaned back against the white pillow. "I don't want to stay here. I want to go home with you," I moaned.

"And I want you home. But Med wants you to stay here for the night, so he can keep an eye on you."

"Med?" I questioned.

"He's a Wolf from the West chapter. A qualified physician, he fixes us when we get messed up. You were adamant about not going to the hospital and there was nowhere else to take you. I knew he'd look after you. But it was close for a while."

"Were you worried?" I asked, looking into his weary face.

"What do you think?" he turned away. I assumed he was going to cry.

"I thought I was going to lose you. I didn't think you'd make it. You lost so much blood, and you wouldn't wake up. Man, I don't know what I'd do without you." He turned back around and faced me. "Promise me you'll never leave me, Dior. Promise me. I couldn't imagine life without you. You're part of me. I've never felt as whole as I do when I'm with you."

I blinked away the tears. "I thought I was going to lose you as well," I said. "When I saw the rifle pointed at your back, I had to do something."

"It was a stupid thing to do," he said.

"Maybe, but you'd do the same for me, wouldn't you?"

He didn't hesitate. "Yes. Yes I would."

"I wasn't planning on getting shot you know. I just wanted to warn you to get out of the way."

Buzz took my hand in his and brought it to his lips. "You saved my life, you know that don't you? I'll never be able to pay you back. Nothing I could ever do will make up for what you've done. But I'll never forget."

I stared into his eyes. "Please, Buzz. Don't ever forget. There might be a time when you'll hate me so much, maybe even want to hurt me; if that time ever comes, remember what you said. No matter what may happen in the future, remember that I love you enough to give my life for you."

"Why are you talking like this, Dior?" He frowned. "I could never hate you."

You wanna bet, I thought.

"I love you," he said.

"And I love you too," I said, giggling through my tears. "Look what a pair we make." I laughed. It hurt.

I took deep breaths. The pain stopped my humor. "You okay?"

I gritted my teeth and shook my head.

"Med!" Buzz yelled.

The Doctor came out of his office shaking his head. "I thought I told you she needs rest. Right now, laughter is not the best medicine."

I watched him put a needle into the bottom of the IV tube. I instantly calmed and felt sleepy. I looked at them watching me as my eye lids became heavy and dropped.

"Night, babe." Buzz's voice came out as a slow, dull tone and echoed through my head. His hand caressed the top of my head as my eyelids closed, and I slept.

I woke up feeling as if I hadn't eaten for days. I was alone and the lamp in the corner of the room gave off an eerie glow. I ached for company, so I called out for Med.

He came out of his room, rubbing his eyes. Dressed in faded jeans and a white T-shirt, this was the kind of man I associated with the Wolves. His well-built arms displayed an impressive array of colorful tattoos. I was glad the white coat was gone. I've never liked doctors much.

"Sorry, did I wake you?" My voice sounded normal now.

"How's the pain?" He asked.

"Bearable," I smiled. "Buzz gone home?"

"No. he's crashing at a brother's place. He wants to be close by. I've never seen him like that before. He was a mess. Begging me and praying to God to save you.

I didn't know he even believed in God. What did you do to the guy, Dior?"

He smiled, but I knew it was said as an accusation. It wasn't the first time someone asked me that. I supposed the Wolves were noticing the change in Buzz.

"I guess you're willing to believe in anything if you need faith," I said.

Med sat with me while I sipped a mug of soup. We talked about the Wolves and he told me about what went on in the West chapter. It didn't sound any different from the Mother chapter. A bunch of brothers who hung out together, got into some trouble, but enjoyed their life. He never mentioned the other side of the Wolves.

I loved listening to him talk. He had so much passion for the bikers' lifestyle. I could have listened to him all night.

"Okay," he said, getting up from his seat. "You'd better get some sleep. Buzz wants you home tomorrow, but I'm not letting you leave unless you have your strength back. You need something to help you sleep?'

"No. All I have to do is close my eyes. You could give me something for the pain. I'd rather not have to wake you, if it starts up again."

He smiled and gave me another injection.

I grabbed his arm as he turned to leave. "Med. Thanks – thanks for everything."

Leaning over, he pinched my cheek. "I can see the attraction," he smiled. "Buzz is a lucky guy, in more ways than one. I hope he knows that."

The medication must have been strong. God knows how I managed to sleep on that hard trolley bed.

I sat on the chair by the desk, rubbing my aching back, chatting to Med as we waited for Buzz to arrive.

I still felt weak, and couldn't stay on my feet for too long. But I managed to get to the bathroom and wash my face. The dark circles under my eyes were almost black against the whiteness of my skin. I looked at my refection and then down at the sink. It suddenly hit me. I could have died. I'd been shot saving a Wolf's life, yet I was alive. But I didn't take the bullet for a Wolf. I took it for Buzz, the man I loved. The thought of not seeing my parents again, or being able to speak to Clay and Beth one last time, made me shiver. Once I was able to ride again, I was going to visit. I owed it to them and myself.

Buzz picked me up in the car; he was silent throughout the journey. I touched his hand and smiled at him.

"What's wrong?" I asked.

"Nothing. I was just thinking…"

I knew what he was thinking. "Hey, it's over. I'm okay."

"Yeah I know, but I can't stop thinking about what if—what if you died. You shouldn't have been put in that position. I don't think I could live without you."

He kept his eyes on the road, but squeezed my hand.

I didn't know what to say to him. I was confused. He didn't want me to leave him, but it was going to happen sooner than later. And once he found out what I'd been doing, playing him, the way he felt about me now would become a forgotten memory.

Twenty minutes into the drive and my shoulder started to pain me. I gritted my teeth and shifted in my seat. The throb quickly turned into a blinding pain, which pulsated harder with each second.

"Medication wearing off?" Buzz asked, concerned.

I nodded and took an intake of breath.

"Hold on," he said, pulling the car over to the side of the road.

Searching through the glove compartment, he pulled out a canister of pills Med had given him.

"Here," he said, handing me one.

"Two," I gasped.

I thought I was going to pass out. Buzz had the same idea, because he gave me another pill without argument, and then held a bottle of water to my lips.

"Do you want to lie down in the back?"

"No. I'll be fine. I want to sit beside you."

It took about ten minutes for the drugs to kick in. I felt drunk. My head was floating and everything moved in slow motion.

"Do you mind if I make a quick stop at the clubhouse?" he asked.

"Nah, I don't mind," I slurred.

Buzz laughed.

I must have dozed off, because when I opened my eyes, we were parked. I shivered as I recalled what happened there the other night.

Buzz opened the door and helped me out. Covering my shoulders with my jacket, we walked up the steps to the club.

The whole of the East chapter was in the bar. Every one of the Wolves clapped. Even Mud joined in. The scene seemed surreal. Mud walked over to me and pinned a small red dot patch on the left arm of my jacket. He didn't have to say anything; I knew what he was feeling. Stepping back, he watched as my brothers and sisters surrounded me with greetings and kisses.

"Not too much pain … I'm good … thanks," I repeated, to every greeting and question that bombarded me.

I was out of it, high on Codeine or whatever it was Buzz had given me. It was bizarre.

Trent and Sly brought the couch out of the office and pushed it against the far wall of the club, and then Buzz and Trent walked me over.

The volume rose to such an extent that Mud told them to keep it down. They admired me and it was strange at the time, I couldn't understand why I was getting special treatment. None of it would sink in. Wolves came over, sat and chatted to me, but not a lot of what they said made any sense. I lay on the couch, with the whole of the club floor in my view, listening and watching my brothers and sisters laughing and drinking.

Trent came over and sat down. Picking up my jacket, his eyes fixated on my new patch.

"What does it represent?" I slurred.

He stared at me, as though I'd said something stupid. "You took a hit for the club," he answered. "Look, Dior, I'm not good at things like this, but I just want you to know—you saved my man's life, and I owe you big. He's my best buddy, so if there's anything you need, you only have to ask. I love that son of a bitch more than anyone."

I thought he was gonna cry.

"I understand," I said, and reached out to touch his arm.

Trent smiled, but then got up and walked away. Displaying emotion was not something he was used to.

I was feeling relaxed, warm, and comfortable. I closed my eyes.

"Keep it down." I heard someone say.

"You've got a good woman there, Buzz. There are not many here that would take a bullet for their man."

I felt a hand caress the top of my head, and then I fell asleep.

***

I was in too much pain to be in awe of the patch or consider what it meant. I'd seen another patch, a red cross, on the back of Mud's jacket, below the Wolf's head. I'd assumed it was just a symbol for being the chief, but now I wasn't so sure. I asked Buzz about it the next day.

"It's a symbol to show the member's killed for the club."

I swallowed hard. I knew whose death Mud was proudly advertising. The thought sickened me.

"Who?" I asked.

"Some member of a rival gang," he shrugged, "It was when the Wolves were just starting out. Mud got five years inside for it."

"Anyone else have the patch? I haven't seen it on your jacket."

He shook his head, lit up a joint and laid his head back on the couch. "I haven't killed anyone; at least I don't think I have. I'm not stupid. You think I want to spend the rest of my life behind bars? I've got too much to lose, especially now."

I visualized the cops cuffing Buzz and putting him in the police car. His eyes pleaded and he called out to me. "Why, Dior? Why?"

My stomach churned, I thought I was going to heave.

"I don't think I'd ever be able to kill anyone," I said, thinking back to the scene in Mud's office.

He lifted his head and gazed at me. "Sometimes it's kill or be killed."

The thought stayed with me all day.

If I were put in that situation, I wouldn't hesitate in firing a gun, whether I was a Wolf or not, I'd protect myself. However, I wasn't a cold blooded killer. Although I wished I was.

I spent the next few days looking carefully at every Wolf's Jacket. I saw the symbolic cross on two other jackets; Saber's and Pug's. It surprised me; I'd never noticed them before, especially Saber's. He was my friend, and I wondered how easy it would be to get him to talk about the murder, maybe even record our conversation. As far as I knew, he'd only had a couple of stints inside, one for robbery and one for G.B.H, which meant he'd gotten away with murder.

*****

If there was any way for a Lady to go up in rank, it was by receiving the red circle. My title didn't change. I'd always be known as Buzz's Lady. I'd never be made an officer of the club, at least not while Mud was running things. Nevertheless, my status changed.

The Wolves respected the patch I wore. They respected me. There were only another two members of the whole club who had been given the honour, an ex-member and Stamp, a member of the South chapter.

It wasn't about being shot, that happened often. It was about giving your life for another brother.

I never paid dues or bought another drink. My bike was fixed free of charge. I never had to ask for anything. No one ordered me around, and when asked, if I said no, they listened. This made it much easier to get the inside information I needed.

Buzz couldn't do enough, and it wasn't just about being worried about my welfare. He was trying to give something back. I knew there would come a time when he could repay me.

I only saw Clay and Beth once while I was injured. I told them I'd had an accident and that the bike was at the shop. Thankfully, they believed me. I doubt they would if I'd told them the truth.

I hadn't seen my parents since my gig in Birmingham, which now seemed like a lifetime ago. At first, I called them every week, and then it was easier not having to talk to them rather than making up new excuses why I couldn't go down. I owed them a visit, but I wasn't ready to face them. Too ashamed of what I'd become, what I'd already done.

Another month passed before I could ride again.

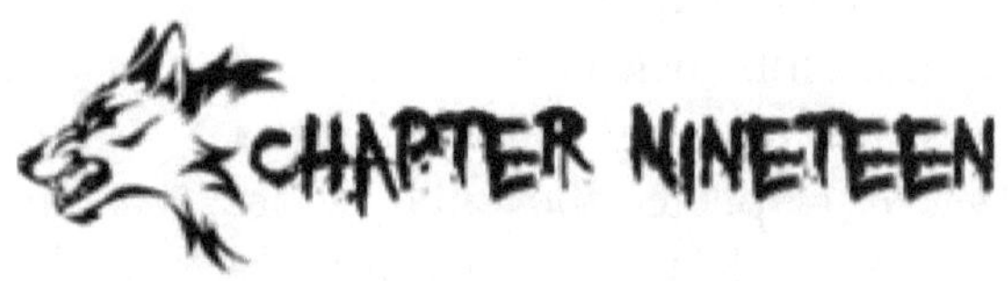

CHAPTER NINETEEN

I couldn't keep a tape on my person in case Buzz found it. His sexual urges were such, I'd never know when he would want to grab and feel me up. I hid a small camcorder in the cellar of the Drunken Squid, and one in the clubhouse office. It was risky going in and changing the disks over after each meeting, and even though I'd had some narrow escapes, I'd yet to be caught in the act. I knew there was a danger the cameras might be discovered, but it would take them too long to figure out who the spy was; I'd be long gone by then.

The Wolves didn't seem to have a problem with me taking photos while we were on a run. They had no idea who was going to see the pictures. I already had a good portfolio of evidence stored at my apartment; photocopies of accounts, records of drug runs and shipments; names that mattered.

I know it was a stupid thing to do, but I'd found a report of a gun sale that was going down that afternoon. The opportunity for getting hard evidence was too good to miss.

How brainless would you have to be to list the time and meeting place and then leave it for all to see? It wasn't exactly lying around. I had to look for it, but it wasn't hard to find.

I wondered what Mud would do with his records if the police suddenly stormed the place one night. Strange, that I'd never known that to happen. I would have thought with the Wolves' track record, the police would have raided the club house at least once a week.

I made sure I was on the dirt track behind the church, well hidden, before anyone showed up. A burgundy Renault Meagan pulled up first. The driver and passenger remained in the car until Saber arrived on a stolen Wide Glide Harley. King followed in a white Mercedes. I don't know why it surprised me to see Saber, maybe it wasn't surprise—maybe it was disappointment. I knew King would be there; he was the Wolves weapons officer after all.

I took my camcorder out of the case and started filming.

The four of them stood behind the car, looking into an open boot. It didn't matter that I couldn't zoom in to get a close up of what was inside, as Saber and King pulled out each gun and examined it in full view of the camera lens. They lined the sight up, pulled the trigger back and aimed. Weighing the guns, as they expertly threw them from one hand to another. Money exchanged hands, and I had it all down on video. I recorded the number plates of both vehicles and of Saber's cycle, which I'd already learnt had been played with, so all evidence of the previous owner, serial numbers and such were filed off.

I stayed hidden for another five minutes after they'd left, before climbing back onto my bike.

I'd just passed the church and was about to ride back through the village when I caught sight of Saber's bike.

My stomach dropped. I reached to grab the camera case, which I thought was hanging from my shoulder, but then remembered I'd put it under my seat. Luckily, I'm a quick thinker and my gift of the gab has gotten me out of many sticky situations. I slowed my bike and stopped beside Saber. He was sitting causally, holding his helmet in the crook of his arm.

Relax, I warned myself. Taking my helmet off, I smiled at him. "Hey, how's it going?"

"Good," he answered. "What you doing this way?" It wasn't an accusation, so I calmed.

"Been visiting," I said, nodding towards the church.

"Oh … Oh," he repeated, catching on. "I'm sorry. Anyone close?"

I had a feeling our conversation would get back to Buzz and maybe even Mud. I had to be very careful about what I said. "My parents are buried there."

"I'm sorry," he said. And he looked it too.

"It's okay; it was a long time ago. They died in a car crash," I added, before he had a chance to ask.

"Hell. That must have been tough."

I shrugged. "What you doing down here?" I asked, deciding to change the subject.

"Had some business to take care of."

I nodded.

"Listen. While we're here - I've got some something else that needs sorting. You wanna come along?"

I looked down at my watch. "I'm supposed to meet Buzz in forty minutes. Will it take long?"

"Not long. To tell you the truth, Dior, I could do with some back up."

"Sure," I said. "Why not. But hey, this is a favour for you. I'd rather Buzz didn't know about this?"

He looked at me strange.

"He doesn't want me doing any business without

his say so. What can I do? The man tells me to jump, I say how high."

Saber grinned. "You got a blade?"

I shook my head. "Am I gonna need one?"

Shit! What had I gotten myself into, I cursed.

"Here, take mine." He reached into his back pocket and gave me his flick knife. "Will you use it?"

"If I have to, yes." I replied.

Putting my helmet back on, I sat on the bike and waited until Saber moved off.

My anxiety increased, as we rode into a tough area of town known for drug dealers. We were wearing our colours so no one harassed us as we parked our bikes beside three blocks of flats and a group of youths. The lads watched us as we walked by, and into one of the blocks. Saber didn't acknowledge them, so I blanked them as well. For a second, I was worried about leaving the bikes outside, but then shrugged it off. You'd have to be mad to touch a Wolf's ride, recalling what happened on the Sheffield run.

The flat looked about twelve floors high, and I hoped we were taking the elevator. No such luck. Saber started climbing the concrete steps. He took two steps at a time, and I had a hard time keeping up with him. Used syringes and discarded beer cans littered the stairway; the stink was strong, a mixture of piss and beer. At the top of the first floor, propped up against the exit door, a drunk called down to us, asking for change. Saber ignored him. I side-stepped, hoping the tramp wouldn't try to make a grab for my ankles.

We climbed up to the second floor and Saber held the door open for me as we went through. The hallway was narrow and over-looked an open balcony. I peered over to see if I could see the bikes, but we were on the opposite side of where we parked. A playground was straight ahead. Another gang of youths was sitting on rusty swings and on faded painted climbing frames. They were staring at me. I stepped away and continued following Saber. He stopped two doors down and knocked twice on the chipped, painted green, wooden door.

He turned to me. "You ready?"

I nodded, and held tightly to the knife in my pocket.

The moment he heard the sound of a chain being pulled across the door, Saber reached under his jacket and pulled out a small, black handgun. I felt sick at the sight of it.

The guy inside, opened the door a crack and when he saw us, tried to slam the door shut. Saber kicked it open. The force knocked the guy to the floor. Saber rushed at him, grabbed him by the scruff of his T-shirt and threw him against the wall. Without a word, he raised the gun and whacked the guy in the face. His left eye opened up and speckled the cream coloured walls with blood.

There were another two people in the room. One woman, crouched on the sofa, her knees hugging her chest and a young guy, I guessed in his early twenties. He stood up and was about to bolt, when I pulled out my knife and flicked the blade out.

"Stay where you are," I warned, holding the knife out. I was ready to use it if need be.

"Time to pay up," Saber growled at the guy that had blood dripping down his face.

"I swear, I was coming down today," the guy cried, through his swelling nose.

"So, where's the money?" Saber asked, raising the gun.

"Under the mattress in the bedroom," The guy on the sofa said.

"Please don't hurt him anymore," the woman cried.

Saber's eyes turned black. "You should be more worried about what I'm gonna do to you," he warned. "Dior, go check the money."

I worried about leaving him with the woman. She wasn't very attractive: even so, I wasn't sure about Saber's taste.

I walked toward the bedroom. "In here?"

The woman nodded her head. Saber stepped away; raising the gun so he'd have a clear shot of all three of them should they try anything.

I'd no idea how much they owed the Wolves, so when I pulled the mattress off the bed and found an assortment of drugs and a wad of notes. I pocketed all the money. Saber didn't say anything about drugs, so I left them. I had a feeling the group would need them.

"Got it," I called out.

I walked back into the living room to see Saber standing over the two on the sofa.

"No one fucks with the Wolves," he said, bringing his hand down hard across the woman's face. "I don't wanna ever have to come here collecting again." He punched the guy in the face, slamming his head against the wall and knocking him out.

Turning, Saber looked at the guy on the floor. "You pay on time or you'll be seeing me again, understand? Let's go," he growled.

I opened the front door, and we walked out.

I was buzzed but ashamed about how I was feeling. I was on a high and felt tough and invincible, as if I could do and get away with anything.

Saber didn't say a word as we walked back down to the ground floor. Before we stepped outside, he turned and held his hand out. I reached into my jacket pocket and pulled out the wad of cash.

"The little shit," he said with a grin, as he counted

out the notes. "Here, take this." He handed me a bundle of 50's.

"I didn't do much," I muttered, and pocketed the money without a thought. Still shocked by what had just gone down.

"You backed me up. That was enough," he said.

As we walked up to the bikes, one of the eldest of the youths called out.

"Henry giving you guys trouble?"

I think he was trying to show off in front of his friends. Proving to them he wasn't afraid to address a Wolf.

Saber's reaction was decisive; he pulled out his gun and aimed it at the boy's head. "Keep your fucking nose out of Wolves' business."

The gang reacted by scuttling back. The youth who dared to address us stood shaking. I didn't blame him. I'd never had a gun pointed at my head, but I could imagine how it felt.

Saber tucked the gun under the waist of his jeans and then climbed on to his bike. We put our helmets on and zipped up our jackets.

"I'll see you later," I yelled to him, before starting up my Harley.

I took a detour to my apartment and stashed the cash away. Every note I was given or earned as a Wolf was dirty money, and for now, I didn't intend to spend any of it.

Saber kept his word, Buzz never learnt about my adventure. I think he was too scared of what he would do to him if he found out.

However, he did hear about the conversation we had.

A couple of days passed. I was standing in the kitchen by the sink when Buzz came in and sat down at the table.

"Dior, I heard about what happened to your parents."

I almost dropped the plate I was cleaning. Thinking how the hell did he find out about me being related to the Tyrants.

"Saber told me," he continued.

I exhaled and my heart started slowing.

"How come you never mentioned it before?" He stood behind me, grabbed my waist, and snuggled his face into my neck.

"It's not something I like to talk about," I answered.

"Yeah, I guess not. So you got any other family? You never talk about them."

I decided to be honest for once.

"My uncle was killed in a fight. He was stabbed."

"Shit," Buzz said, swinging me around to face him. Soap suds landed on his shirt and covered the floor.

"My brother committed suicide," I continued.

"Hell, Babe." He looked both shocked and concerned.

"Yeah, he killed himself when he found out our uncle was really his father and he'd been murdered."

"Shit, Dior, I'm so sorry."

Pulling me away from the sink, he sat me down at the kitchen table. I wiped my hands on my jeans. I wasn't about to cry. I'd done enough of that.

"Jeez, you've had it rough. How can anyone stay sane after so much grief?"

I stared at him, as though he'd just said something profound.

"You don't know the half of it."

"Then tell me," he begged. "I'm here for you, babe."

"One day. One day, I'll sit you down and tell you everything. I promise. But not yet. I'm not ready. It's still raw."

"Okay, I understand. No – shit, I don't understand. Nothing's ever hurt me like that."

I nodded and hugged him tightly, while my stomach

churned. Grief eats you up. It's inside of you, slowly chewing away every emotion until you stop feeling. I'd been carrying my grief around since I found out the truth. It never left me. It never gave me a moment's peace. I couldn't get on with my life because I was living a life caused by my grief. Only vengeance was keeping me sane. It was driving me on every day. I think if I didn't have a goal to work on, something to occupy my mind, I would have joined Dylan and John a long time ago.

My anger was boiling and I couldn't look at Buzz any more. He'd dredged up old emotions, and I didn't want to hate him for something his family did. If only he knew.

Hugging me, he caressed my hair and then lifted up my chin with the tip of his finger. "It's okay. I'm here anytime you want to talk. I promise you, Dior, life is going to be different for you. I'm going to make you happy. Things will get better."

He kissed me lightly on the lips. I opened my mouth; I wanted to taste his tongue. A tear dripped down my face as he slowly pulled my top over my head. We made love on the kitchen table; slow, sensual intercourse. For a while, Buzz allowed me to forget my problems.

***

Three days passed when I finally got the opportunity to chat to Saber alone. I just popped into the Drunken Squid on my way back from the library, where I was putting my investigation into a neat report.

Jem and Sly were sitting in the corner of the pub, deep in conversation. I waved my hand in greeting. Saber was leaning over the bar chatting to Tray. I walked over and said "hi." Tray asked me how I was doing and Saber bought me a Bud. I waited until Tray went out the back before striking up a conversation with the Wolf.

Reaching into my jacket pocket, I pressed the small button on the recording device I had hidden; state of the art microfilm, capable of picking up to three hours of crisp recording. I wasn't too worried about carrying around a recording device now. I was a trusted patch. There was no reason a Wolf would search me.

"You know what happened the other day," I said.

Saber turned his head toward me.

"I doubt it's gonna be the last time I'm asked to back someone up, and next time I want to be prepared."

"What you after?" he asked.

"I was thinking about getting a gun. Just a small handgun, you know, one I can carry in my pocket. Any ideas where I can get one from?"

"Yeah, sure. You know what you're after?"

"Not really." I smiled.

"You should speak with King, he'll hook you up."

"I'd rather this was between just the two of us. I can't explain, but I'd rather just deal through you."

He looked at me with a puzzled expression. I thought I'd pushed it too much; maybe I should have used Buzz as an excuse.

He shrugged. "Sure, I can set you up with something. Just give me a couple of days."

"Thanks." I breathed a sigh of relief.

"You ever shoot a gun?" He asked.

"No. But I'm a fast learner. How hard can it be?"

He smiled. "Harder than it looks. Some handguns have a powerful kick to them, hold them wrong, and it can split your hand open. I can help you if you want. I'll set up some targets and teach you how to shoot."

"That would be great thanks, Saber. So, you're a bit of an expert when it comes to guns?"

"Not really, that's King's bag. But I've had some

experience." He winked and then called Tray over and ordered another round. I paid for this one.

"You ever shoot a gun, for real, I mean?"

"Yeah, plenty of times."

"You ever shoot anyone?" I laughed to make a joke out of it.

"Yeah," he answered.

I spluttered in my beer glass. "Really, shit, what happened?"

Saber didn't hesitate in telling me about the murder. He was proud to talk to such a captivated audience. My gasps and comments made him presume I was in awe of his actions. He then indicated the red cross on his jacket. I caressed the patch feigning admiration.

We laughed and talked about other times he'd shot his gun, and not just warning shots. I was an avid listener and said all the right things to keep him talking.

I had it all on tape.

Apparently, his victim, a lone biker, had been mouthing and throwing his weight around the Drunken Squid. The Wolves had warned him more than once to keep it closed. I wondered why they put up with him, if anyone behaved like that now they'd be battered before being thrown out. But then the biker made a big mistake. He started bragging around town that he was going to get patched in, and that once patched, it wouldn't be long until he'd become an officer. But it wasn't the biker's arrogance that got him killed. If he'd left it as just talk, he'd probably still be alive. Well, that's what I told myself. When Mud learnt the biker was dealing using the Wolves' name and pocketing the cash without notifying the club about the sideline, Mud ordered the hit.

The poor biker thought he was being patched in; instead, Saber drove him to a forest and shot him execution style-- bullet in the head. The body was still buried somewhere underneath forest debris.

After his confession, I changed the subject. Although there was plenty I wanted to ask him, I didn't want to push it.

I phoned Saber the next day, told him to forget about getting me a gun for the time being. I said I was worried how Buzz would react if I didn't ask him first. Saber said Buzz would be cool about it, and was surprised I didn't already have a piece. I must have left him with an impression that I went on daily pick-ups. Luckily, he understood and said he'd sort me out when I was ready.

I expected Buzz to present me with a handgun. I'd already learnt that Saber was a blabber mouth.

I erased some of our conversations, anything that would have made me look bad. All I needed was the confession.

CHAPTER TWENTY

Another run to Matlock. This time for a bikers' festival. Food, bands, beer, bikers, what more could one ask for?

During the run down, we stopped at a pub for refreshments. Trouble wasn't on our mind, but things happen when you're in such a large group. A wrong look from a customer, or a silent gesture could kick off an argument ending in a bar fight. What enraged the Wolves the most was having their name disrespected. Whether people knew of us or not, our patch gave us status and a demand for respect. Most of the fights were between the male members, but the Lady Wolves were far from being saints.

I only started a fight if I felt I had something to prove.

Mud once told me to pick a fight with another female biker. I refused and said if he wanted her on the floor, he could do it himself. Luckily, he laughed it off. Jem came up to me later that evening and told me how surprised she was that I'd gotten way with talking to him like that. I shrugged, like it was no big deal, but I knew from experience that you didn't say no to Mud.

Half of me wanted to see how far I could push him and see how Buzz acted if Mud started. Instead, I kept my distance.

It was on the Matlock run that a lone, female biker felt the brunt of my jealous rage.

We didn't care what sort of pub we took over as long as the beer was cold and the place was empty. Empty, because of the size of our group. We didn't want to end up standing squashed between regular customers. The amount of vehicles parked in front of the pub told Mud, whether or not the place was suitable.

The landlord didn't know what to make of us as we piled into the Hog's Head's lounge. I knew he wasn't going to ask us to leave. First, he wasn't about to turn away customers who looked as though they were bound to drink a lot in a short time. Second, no one told the Wolves to leave.

I knew she was trouble the moment she walked into the pub. Karen didn't have to warn me about her. She was already in my sights, as well as most of the Wolves.

She wanted a piece of the action. That was obvious. Why else would the female biker stop for a drink in the same bar we happened to be at? Maybe it was paranoia, but I had a feeling she'd been following us, waiting for us to stop somewhere. I'd seen it happen too often.

Wearing tight leathers and a black helmet in the crook of her arm, she leaned over the bar and ordered a beer. It didn't take long for a Wolf to slide up beside her and start chatting.

She was safe. They wouldn't try anything. As long as she stayed away from a Lady's man, she'd be leaving the bar in one piece. Although there were plenty of looks from the Wolves that told me if she had walked into our club house, she'd be on the pool table with her legs wide open by now.

Was she safe from me? I was pissed that she'd walked into our party without an invite and was getting the Wolves' attention. I was the top dog, so to speak, and not just because I was Buzz's Lady. I had the looks, body, and attitude that went with the title. I was jealous. She was striking, with long chestnut hair, slim, sexy legs and a pretty face. She made me feel ugly.

I stayed by Buzz and made sure I had all his attention. A group of Ladies walked over toward us and started bitching about the biker. I think they expected me to take care of it. Buzz laughed and then walked over to play pool with Trent.

I came out of the toilets to find the bitch leaning against the pool table talking and flirting with my man. Maybe I was overreacting, but the Ladies were watching, and I knew I had to act. My stomach was in knots as I walked over to them. I was holding a glass of beer in my left hand, and my right was clenched in a fist. I stood in front of her and slowly poured the pint over her head. Gasps, cheers, and whistles informed me that my action was acceptable. Buzz stepped back but still got beer on him. He glared at me, and then looked at the soaked biker, smiled and walked away.

"Jesus Christ," she screeched, wiping the beer from her soaked face. "What the hell did you that for?"

"You've outstayed your welcome," I told her.

"What's your fucking problem?" she yelled.

I belted her in the face, and she fell to the floor.

Not one Wolf went to her aid. They wouldn't have dared.

"Get up," I yelled.

She gingerly got to her feet and stood in front of me while pinching her bleeding nose. She didn't look so attractive now, I thought.

"I'd advise you to turn around and walk out that fucking door and God help you if we ever meet again."

She turned and looked at the Wolves, who were watching, most with grins on the faces. Walking past me, she took her helmet and jacket from the bar and left the pub.

I took a deep breath while the volume of conversation rose. I was still raging and needed to vent my anger. I looked around for Buzz and saw him standing beside Saber and Karen. I grinned, and he smiled back.

I went up to him, took his hand, and pulled him out of the bar. He knew what I wanted, and if he felt the need to chat to another female, I knew what he needed.

We had sex around the back of the pub, up against the wall.

"Nothing would have happened," he said, as we re-adjusted our clothing. "She didn't do anything for me. Why would she, when I've got you?"

He grabbed me and cupped my chin, forcing me to look into his face.

"I love you, Dior."

My stomach did butterflies. I felt excited, but also worried. I loved him and yet I was stabbing him in the back; getting inside info on the Wolves, ready to send them all to jail.

It was a wake up call. I was a Wolf and I loved my brothers, the respect, and the lifestyle, but then again, it was all make-believe wasn't it? I was beginning to believe the hype.

I smiled at him. "I didn't think you would. The bitch just needed a lesson in etiquette."

He laughed.

I caught Mud staring at me as we walked back inside.

***

Although I'd been on a few runs, this one was very different. By the time we got to Matlock, the place was already busy. The festival, which was held every year, was a big deal.

Bikers journeyed far to be part of the festivities. Because of the amount of patches on show, the place was policed; so much we couldn't walk around with a joint between our fingers.

Buzz asked me to make a special effort with my appearance and on arrival at the festival, I understood why. There was a lot of competition. Not just for the Wolves, but for me as well. The jeans and leather clad women were gorgeous. Not the average dogs you'd usually see riding with a crew. Whether they were tough, I didn't know, and had no intention of finding out. It was a party and I was going to enjoy myself.

My hair hung loose, curled at the tips. I had on tight leather trousers and a leather bra top. Heavy, silver jewellery finished off my outfit. The weather was lovely. If I was going to take my jacket off any time during the day, I wanted something to show for it, and a thirty-eight bust was certainly going to get me attention. The rest of the Lady Wolves also made an effort, making a hundred and fifty plus strong patched bikers' gang a talking point.

I noticed the Warlocks straight away. Their famous patch stood out among the sea of bikers.

There were no parking spaces available, surrounding the festival, and as we wanted to keep our bikes together, we did a circuit around where the event was, parked five minutes away and then walked down.

The atmosphere was something else. Roar of motorbikes, excited chatter and laughter, and the background base of rock music filled the air. Stalls selling memorabilia, gothic jewelry, and CD's lined up along the field, which had been rented for the event. Traders of bike gear, parts, and clothing added to the bikers' market. People milled around the stalls, some just browsing, others looking to buy.

There was a lot of money to be made at these festivals. Plenty of food vendors kept the bikers happy. Everything from fish and chips, hotdogs, jacket potatoes, and fried chicken was available. Ice cream, doughnuts, cold beverages, and cafeterias had also been set up. The aroma of food was making my mouth water.

Beer tents, too many to count. But you'd never see a biker staggering around drunk. They knew what their alcohol limit was.

Once we entered the centre and made our presence felt, we separated. Some of the chapters stayed together in their group, but no one walked around with less than five of their brothers. It was too dangerous. We separated from Mud and hung with Trent, Saber, Sly, Jem and Karen.

Buzz knew many of the bikers, and we stopped and chatted as we slowly made our way through the throng. I had a feeling I knew where he was heading, but it took nearly half an hour before reaching our destination. Guitars and vocals became louder, the closer we got.

There were two entertainment tents, no one famous, but they were talented. They would have to be; the festival wasn't the place for amateur musicians. One tent was blasting out some heavy thrash, which has never been my scene, so I directed our group to the other one. Four musicians, as well as the lead singer, were belting out a Guns & Roses number. Buzz knew how much I was itching to get onto the stage and jam. He grinned while I rocked with the audience.

When Trent returned from the bar with the beers, we found a space in the audience and moved closer to watch the band. We stayed for about half an hour, until it got too warm and crowded.

Beer was served cold and it was a good job as well. When we left the band tent, the festival was bursting.

It was difficult to find a free patch of grass to sit and chill. The sun was beating down, and it wasn't long until we removed our jackets to display impressive tattoos among other things. Buzz had a black skull painted on his left arm, an Eddie—Iron Maiden mascot—painted on the top of his right arm. On the front of his left wrist was the green and blue rattle snake, which he had done the same time I had my tattoo. Trent displayed a tough tattoo across his neck, which looked like a barbed wire necklace. Sly and Saber's arms were inked out— no skin left to tattoo.

We were having a browse around the traders' stalls, when Buzz's mobile rang. The rest of us were too busy checking out the T-shirts on sale to wonder about the call.

He soon got our attention.

"Get back to the bikes quick," he ordered. "Split up and get back to London. If there's any cops near the bikes, walk away. Don't wear your colours until you're out of the town. Fuck! Don't wear your jackets at all."

"What's the deal?" Trent whispered, as he looked over his shoulder.

"Hue and Ruban have messed up two young girls. The cops are gonna be gunning for the Wolves."

Jem, Karen, and I quickly bought a T-shirt each from a stall, and then we split up. Without making it obvious, we hurried back to our bikes. Buzz made calls, alerting everyone of the pending trouble. Between his phoned warnings, I asked what he meant by messed up.

"What do you think?" he answered curtly.

I didn't want to think.

"The stupid fucks!" He cursed.

"How young were these girls?"

"Too young," he said.

"Where's Hue and Ruben?" I hoped they'd already been arrested.

"They took off."

His phone rang again.

"The police have got Mud and five others in custody," he told me, after closing the phone.

There were around thirty bikes still parked up. I ran over to mine pulled the seat up and jammed my jacket inside.

"What do you want to do?" I asked.

"Nothing. They can take care of themselves. We're leaving."

I nodded and started up my bike. "Straight home?"

"Yeah. Stay behind me in case I need to stop."

I gave a salute and then pulled out behind him.

We were some distance from the festival but could already see a roadblock ahead. We could have ridden straight through, but Buzz didn't want to take the chance. I followed him as we made a detour across fields and footpaths.

I don't know if he knew where he was going. I just followed. My mind was somewhere else.

Too young, he had said. How messed up were they? Raped, beaten, probably. But they were well enough to contact the police to give a statement, maybe even identify the rapist in a line up. Boy was I tempted to call up the cops and give their names. I think Ruben was the ginger haired Wolf from the West chapter. Hue had long, curly blonde hair, greased back and tied in a ponytail. He had the same build as most of the Wolves. But luckily, a noticeable facial feature. Hue had a harelip; a birth defect that looked more like a war scar. He was easy to identify.

We took a few more detours before reaching London. By the time we'd gotten back to Buzz's apartment, I was shattered and frozen.

We hadn't made one stop, and although we weren't going flat out, riding a motorbike down a motorway without a jacket was a dangerous thing to do.

Once home, he made some calls and learnt that Mud and the others had been released. It looked as though Hue and Ruben had gotten away with it. For now.

I had no intention of letting it drop. Both were going to be named as the rapists at the Matlock festival. The guys weren't planning on leaving the country. It could wait, but they were going down.

CHAPTER TWENTY-ONE

I had enough evidence to put most of the Wolves inside for a long time. The date for my departure wasn't crossed out on a calendar or anything. I had no idea when it would end. I just kept collecting evidence and living the lie.

I was sitting in my apartment, watching a recording of the previous club meeting. I thought it strange that there was only Mud and two other Wolves present in the office. It was supposed to be an officers' meet, and yet Buzz, Trent, and the others were not there.

Jive, the club's drug officer was sitting next to Smith, president of the South chapter. Mud sat behind his desk. I could tell from their grave expressions that they were about to have a serious discussion. Turning up the volume, I curled my feet up and leaned back in the couch. I never took a drag of my lit cigarette, too stunned by what I heard.

A biker, known as Dave, was playing on the Wolves' ground. Mud planned to wipe out the competition. The guy had been selling drugs on the Wolves turf and

Smith didn't like that. They discussed where and when the hit would take place. Jive and Smith were going to be the executioners. The killing was going to take place in five days.

I turned the DVD off and sat back on the couch, unable to feel or think. My hands were shaking as I lit up another cigarette.

It was time to take the evidence I had, and put it to good use. It was time to walk away.

Five days wasn't a long time to tie up loose ends. Most of the evidence I'd collected had been typed up in a neat report, but I still had some work to do on it.

Shit! I wasn't ready. I hated to admit it, but the Wolves were my family. I loved the lifestyle. I loved riding with them. I'd experienced the worst, but also the best days of my life while being a member of the Wolves. Could I just walk away? It sounded easy enough, but these were my friends and some of them loved and treated me like a sister. I didn't want to stab them in the back, but unfortunately, most of their names came up in the report, including Buzz's.

God helped me but I loved that guy. A love so deep that my stomach turned to knots just thinking about what I was going to do to him.

I had seen the other side to Buzz. He could be a mean son of a bitch, but that was the Wolf in him. A personality he'd been forced to live with. The moment of Mud's release from prison, he distanced himself from the club, and we spent a lot of time together, getting to know each other's likes and dislikes. And he loved me. I believed that, but there was always the deadly secret between us.

I was afraid of what he would do. How he would react when he found out what I'd done. My sudden disappearance would make me an immediate suspect.

However, I couldn't remain and act the part while I watched my brothers fall.

I didn't think the problem would be that I'd betrayed the Wolves; I knew he wanted out of the gang lifestyle. The problem would be that I'd betrayed him; lied and deceived him. I'd played him for a fool, and l knew he'd never forgive me. I would never forgive myself.

I didn't want to send Buzz to jail. He wasn't the same violent, malicious man I'd thought he was when I first met him. If he was still participating in the Wolves' illegal activities freely, I wouldn't think twice about turning him in. But I knew how he felt. I knew he wanted out. Yet, the evidence I collected had Buzz's name written all over it.

Yes, he was a criminal, but that was his past. I had to make a decision, but I was terrified about my choices.

In the two years I'd been a Wolf, Buzz never learnt that I worked as a freelance journalist. That was one secret, which was easy to keep.

I had no intention of walking into a police station and handing the evidence over to the desk sergeant. I didn't want my name associated with the Wolves or the infiltration. And unless I stood up in court and testified against them, the Wolves would never have evidence that it was me who'd betrayed them. Mum's own experience taught me that it wasn't worth the risk. I didn't want to spend the rest of my life looking over my shoulder and living a lie like my parents did. The battle ended with my heart winning.

***

"Okay, I'm listening, what's the big emergency?" Buzz asked, coming up behind me and hugging me around my waist.

"I need to tell you something. You'd better sit down.

No—I'm not pregnant, so you can get that look off your face."

"Thank God, he said," throwing himself down on the couch. "It's not that I don't want kids. I'm just not ready yet. I want you and me to spend time together, get to know each other better before a kid comes into our lives."

I swallowed the bile as I sat beside him. I wished I was drunk or stoned; it would have been a lot easier. "You're not going to like what you hear, but let me finish before you say anything."

"I don't like the sound of this." He wasn't smiling anymore.

"I suppose the easiest way is to tell you from the beginning." I stood up and walked away from the couch. I didn't want to be in hitting distance.

"My real name is Sofi, I am the daughter of Jade and Marcus, ex members of the Tyrants ..."

I told him everything, but I couldn't look at him until I'd finished.

He sat forward, with his head between his legs. "Buzz?"

"Are you done?" He asked, almost in a whisper. Lifting his head up, he started at me. It was pure hatred. "You used me to get to Mud?"

"At first, yes." I wanted to be honest. "But then against my better judgement, I fell in love with you."

"Love! You don't know what love is. If you loved someone, you wouldn't have betrayed them, lied to them for this long."

"You think it was easy?" I yelled. "You don't know how difficult these past two years have been. I've hated living this lie, split between my love for you and my brothers and the hatred for your dad and what the Wolves represent."

"How dare you call them your brothers!" he stood up and took a step towards me. Spittle flew from his mouth and his eyes turned dark. "You're a Bitch. You know that. Those guys would have bled for you. They trusted you and all the time you were playing them. Playing me!"

My heart was breaking, I cursed myself for not leaving a note, but I needed to be honest with him, if for the last time.

"I should have realised you were too good to be true. What a fucking fool I've been."

"Jesus, Buzz, I'm here now, telling the truth, giving you the opportunity to run, before the shit hits the fan. I love you too much to see you end up in jail."

I wanted to get close, to hold him, and reassure him that my love wasn't false, but I was too scared of what he would do to me if I got near.

"So, you've got the evidence, what now? You're gonna walk away, while the rest of your brothers, your friends go down. How can you be so callous? I never saw you as a heartless bitch before."

His words stabbed me. The pain in my heart was unbearable. I felt sick.

"I'm not heartless," I cried. "Why do you think I'm telling you all this. It's because I had a heart, but it belongs to you, it always has. You're not the same vicious Wolf I met two years ago. You are a good person, just a little mixed up. You've changed. I know who you really are. I think you've always been looking for a way out. Now I've given it to you."

"A way out! You have me fucking running from the law, not to mention the Wolves. Do you know what's going to happen when the truth comes out? They're gonna hunt you down, and if I take off, I'm going to look just as guilty. So, what's the evidence anyhow?" he shrugged. "What do you think you have on us?"

"Everything." I answered. "Tape recordings of club meetings, photos, filmed evidence of gun and drug trafficking, records and accounts that date back years, and taped confessions."

His face turned white. He sat back down on the couch and bowed his head. Then he looked up at me, his eyes pleading. "But it's not too late, you can stop this…"

I shook my head "I've already given my report and all the evidence to my editor at the newspaper."

"You stupid fucking bitch." He ran at me.

I backed up against the wall and he stared at me in disgust. I knew he was capable of putting his hands around my neck and throttling me. But I deserved whatever punishment he gave. Tears ran down my face, but I couldn't wipe them away as he had pinned my arms to my side. I stared back at the man I loved.

"Remember I told you there would be a time when you would hate me enough to want to kill me, a time for you to remember that I love you enough to take a bullet for you. To die for you."

Letting go of my arms, he stepped back. His face softened.

"Buzz, please believe me. I love you. I never wanted to hurt you. It killed me to lie to you. I don't want anything to happen to you. If there was a way I could keep your name out of this, I would, but you're involved too much. You have to run, now."

"Oh, shit, Dior, Sofi, whatever your bloody name is, what the fuck have you done?"

I felt it was safe enough to move closer, so I stepped up to him and caressed his check, wiping away a fallen tear.

"I'm so sorry, Buzz," I cried. "I never wanted to hurt you, please believe me."

Haunting silence, and then he spoke again. "What about you," he asked gently. "Where will you go?"

I shrugged. "I don't know. I haven't thought that far ahead. I didn't think it would end so quickly. I recorded Mud, Jive and Smith discussing a hit on a dealer in town. I had to act. I wouldn't be able to live with myself if I let it slide. I knew this time would come, but I'm not ready."

I allowed the tears to fall. I wouldn't turn away from him. I wanted to keep the memory of his beautiful face in my heart and mind forever.

"They'll never stop looking for you. Once they figure out you're the informer. You know that don't you?"

I nodded. "That's for me to worry about."

His eyes darkened as he tilted his head to the side. "So that's it. I don't have any say in this. I'm not allowed to worry about you anymore, is that it?"

"Worry about yourself," I answered. "You have to get away. I can't bear to think about you behind bars. I'm so sorry. I'm sorry I got involved in all this. I'm sorry I met the Wolves. I'm sorry I lied to you, but I'm not sorry about falling in love. I'll never forget what we've shared. What you've meant to me. But it's best this way."

Buzz pulled me to him, we embraced and cried. Neither of us wanted to pull away.

"Come with me," he whispered.

Relief washed over me. "What?"

"Come with me, let's leave together. I can protect you."

"Are you serious?" I asked, looking him in the eyes. "Do you know what you're saying?"

"Yes. And it makes perfect sense. I want to be with you, I can't imagine leaving without you."

"Oh, Buzz, I didn't dare hope you would say those words. I… thought you'd hate me."

"Hate you?" he smiled. "I'm angry, but I understand why you did it. What I don't understand is why you stayed, after I put you through shit, what you went through. Was your need for vengeance so bad?"

He grabbed hold of my hand and squeezed it tightly.

"Yes. It took over my life. I thought about walking away many times, but I couldn't. After what Mud did to my family. I wanted to right the wrongs. I wanted to destroy the Wolves."

"And that included me?"

"If there was any other way…"

"What you've done is stupid and dangerous. I'm angry, I won't deny that, but I can imagine how difficult these past two years must have been for you, living with your guilt. It must have been tearing you apart."

I nodded.

"But, Sofi, I love you too much to hate you."

Fresh tears were falling, but this time they were from happiness.

"Yes. I will leave with you. The thought of not seeing you again, ending what we had, was killing me."

We hugged and kissed each other's wet lips and faces. Then my mobile rang, interrupting our tender moment.

"Shit! The stupid fuck. I'll kill him," I growled, after closing the phone.

"What's happened?" Buzz asked.

"I'll tell you later, we have to pack and get the hell out of town now."

Rushing into the bedroom, we started shoving clothes into rucksacks. We didn't have the time to pack things away and leave the boxes in storage. We didn't have time to raid the bathroom for toiletries. We had to disappear. For all I knew the police could already be on their way over.

"I need to stop off at my apartment to get something." I told him, as we climbed onto his bike.

I knew Buzz' bank account was healthy, but the police would have a warrant out for his arrest and unless we got to the nearest cash machine and withdrew the money immediately, the account might be frozen. I had no idea how much I had stashed back at my apartment, but I knew it was enough not to have to worry about money for quite a while.

After stopping at my place, I told Buzz I had to see my parents to explain what I'd done. I couldn't leave without seeing them one last time. It was too risky to stop off and see Beth and Clay. We had to get out of London fast. I was going to call them later that night and explain what happened. I hoped they would understand, but I knew Clay would never forgive me for not saying goodbye.

CHAPTER TWENTY-TWO

I saw Mum peeking through the cream blinds as we pulled up onto the drive. Dad then had a look. It wasn't until we were standing outside their house, that I considered how they'd react, seeing me on the back of a Wolf's bike. I realised we'd been riding still wearing our colours.

"Better leave our jackets on the bike," I suggested.

I knocked on the door, but there was no answer.

"I know you're in there," I shouted. "Let me in."

I turned to Buzz. He looked anxious. I was getting angry.

"Open the door will you. I haven't got time for this shit. I need to talk to you both, now," I shouted.

"Dad, please," I begged. "I'm in a lot of trouble. Please open the door."

Buzz crouched, opened the letter box and shouted through the gap. "I'm not here to cause trouble. Please open the door and let us in."

He stepped away from the door as it opened.

Dad stared at me, and then looked Buzz up and down before stepping aside and allowing us in the house.

Mum was waiting for us in the living room.

I stepped back in shock when I saw her. "Jesus Christ. Put the fucking gun down," I yelled. "We're not armed."

She lowered the weapon.

"What the hell are you doing bringing a Wolf into my home?" Mum shouted.

"I've done something really stupid, and I'm in trouble."

My parents sat down on the couch. Buzz stayed by the living room door in case he needed to make a quick getaway. I stood by the fireplace. My mouth dried up and no words would come out. Fortunately, Buzz stepped in.

"I want you to know I'm sorry about what happened to your brother. I'm a Wolf, but you have to know it's not by choice. My father forced me into the gang lifestyle. I'm not saying I'm a saint. Far from it, but I'm learning, thanks to Dior… sorry, Sofi. The violence and illegal stuff I've been involved in were done in the Wolves' name. Sofi experienced what a shit I was, but she saw past all that and made me realize I can change. I hope you can give me the benefit of the doubt. I love your daughter and I swear to you, I'll protect her."

Dad turned and faced Buzz. "That's all well and good, but you tell me what the hell you'll be protecting her from," he growled.

I sat down on the couch beside Mum and looked at them. "I changed my lifestyle and moved to London because I needed to get in with the right people, to associate in the right circles. I went to London to find Dylan's killer."

"My God," Mum gasped. "What were you thinking?"

"Jade, let her finish," Buzz urged.

"My plan was to get in with the Wolves and then, when I got the chance, kill Mud."

"You bloody idiot," Dad spat.

"You don't know the half of it," I said.

Buzz stood behind me. His hand rested on my shoulder. I needed the comfort. He gave me the strength to continue.

"I haven't got time to go into details, but I'm sure you have an idea of what I went through to become a trusted member of the gang. I'm not proud of the stuff I've done, and I nearly walked away a couple of times. But my grounds for vengeance increased. And there was no way I was leaving until I'd done what I'd come to do."

"You killed him?" Mum gasped.

"No." Buzz answered for me. "If you think Sofi is capable of cold-blooded murder then you don't know her at all."

I looked up at him and smiled.

He continued. "Although London would be a better place without him."

"I had the opportunity," I said. "But I couldn't go through with it. I came up with another way. I wanted to hurt him bad. I wanted to take away the empire he'd worked hard building. I wanted to destroy the Wolves."

Taking out a packet of cigarettes from my jacket pocket, I offered them around, and then lit my own.

"I started taping conversations about their drug dealings and other illegal transactions. I photocopied accounts, logs, addresses of all their contacts and suppliers. I kept records of the original serial numbers of the stolen bikes. I even took photos and films of illegal firearm sales. This is what I'm good at, and I knew what to look for."

"And you did this without getting caught?" Dad asked. "Didn't you realize how dangerous it was?"

"There were a couple of close encounters. But no one suspected a thing."

"Sofi was shown more respect by the gang then some of the officers. We allowed her to sit in on club meetings. No female has ever been allowed to do that. She tagged along on drug runs, and worked the phone lines for the shop. Our whole operation was at her fingertips. None suspected her."

I nodded. "The Wolves are outlaws in every sense of the word, and I wanted to put them behind bars."

"Except him," Dad said, waving a finger at Buzz.

"Buzz was no better than the rest of them. When Mud was inside, Buzz was the worst of the pack. However, I noticed another side to his personality. It's like you said, Mum. The Tyrants were good people behind closed doors. When Mud returned as president, Buzz started to distance himself from the club. We spent time together as a couple and I fell in love with him. Knowing what I was planning to do, I couldn't let him take the fall, so I told him everything."

Dad and Mum turned and looked at Buzz.

He stood casually, with his hands in his jean pockets. "Yeah, I admit it, I wanted to belt her when she told me, and I nearly did. But I didn't touch her, I swear," he quickly added. "Sofi had given me the opportunity to walk away from the Wolves. The evidence she had on me would have put me away for a long time. I admire her. She went through a lot of shit, probably more than anyone could have coped with, and that took a lot of courage. She told me about the Tyrants, and what you two went through. I can see where she gets her strength. Once everything comes out, there'll be a warrant out for my arrest. I can't come back here, and I can't leave Sofi."

"You're not thinking of running away with him are you?" Mum cried.

"I have no choice," I said. "I didn't want to go to the police with the evidence, so I used my connection at the paper."

I looked around for an ashtray, but couldn't find one. I forgot my parents didn't smoke. "Sorry," I said, and flicked the ash in my hand. Taking a long drag on my cigarette, I continued.

"I wrote up a detailed report on my investigation, and then gave it to my editor at the newspaper. I put the boxed up evidence onto his desk and told him I'd infiltrated the Wolves, and that he could do what he wanted with the evidence. Print it if he wanted, or go to the authorities, but under no circumstances was he to use my name. I figured that way, the Wolves wouldn't have any proof it was me, and I'd be able to fade into the background. There was no way I was going to stand up in court and give evidence against them, not after what you went through, Mum. I wasn't going to spend the rest of my life looking over my shoulder, having a death threat hanging over my head. I'm not about to change my lifestyle or who I am."

"So what happened?" Dad asked.

"I'm guessing the editor couldn't handle the responsibility. He went to the police, handed everything over, including my name as the informant."

"Christ," Mum gasped.

"So you're going to have to testify against the Wolves?" Dad shook his head.

"I'm going to be subpoenaed, so I'd have no choice."

"There'll be a warrant out for her arrest when she doesn't show up," Buzz said.

"You're gonna run?" Mum asked.

"I have no option. You two should understand this. I can't face them in court, and it's not just about what will happen if I did. Some of them were my brothers. They were there when I needed them, and now I've stabbed them in the back. I can't face them."

"Not all the Wolves are bad," Buzz said. "It was a

lifestyle they needed, but when things got dangerous they were in too deep to walk away."

"I wish there was a way to keep Buzz's and their names out of this, but the evidence involves the whole gang."

"Where are you going to go?" Mum asked. Tears glistened as she fought back her emotions.

"All that we need is on the back of our bike. We're going to hit the open road and see where it leads."

"They're gonna be looking for you everywhere. You know that don't you?" Mum cried.

"We'll be careful," I said.

"You'll have to let us know where you are, so we can come and visit," Dad said.

Buzz put his hand on my Dad's shoulder. "I doubt we'll be in one place for too long. But we'll be honoured if you come down and ride with us."

"They don't ride anymore," I said.

"Well—I'll make an exception in this case," Dad said. Mum's smile lit up her face.

"If it's the only way I'm going to see my daughter again, I'd better start looking for a motorcycle."

"Guess I'd better buy a new jacket." Mum grinned.

I was running from the law with my outlaw boyfriend. We were going to have the Wolves hunting us down. I was saying goodbye to my home, my family, and friends, and yet I was feeling happiness that a handful of uppers couldn't produce.

I climbed onto the back of Buzz's bike, waved goodbye to my parents, and held on tightly as he kicked the bike into gear.

We were outlaw bikers in name, in blood.

"You ready babe?" he called.

"Burn rubber," I yelled.

We had each other. We had our bike. Nothing else mattered.

ABOUT THE AUTHOR

Karina Kantas is an award-winning author of fourteen titles. Including The OUTLAW series and the YA fantasy duology, Illusional Reality. She also writes short stories and when her imagination is working overtime, she writes thought-provoking dark flash fiction.

There are many layers to Karina's writing style and voice, as you will see in her flash fiction collection, Heads & Tales and in Undressed she opens up more to her fans, giving them another glimpse into her warped mind.

When Karina isn't busy working on her next bestseller, she's a publicist, author manager and VA. She's also a radio host on the Artist First Radio Network and is YouTuber, podcaster, BookTuber and has won numerous International Film-Festival awards for her trailers and documentary. She is the host of the YouTube show, Behind The Pen. And is also of official graphic designer for the indie media platform Go Indie Now.

Karina writes in the genres of fantasy, MC romance, Young Adult. sci-fi, horror, thrillers and comedy, romance, PNR, dystopian and erotica, dark mafia romance.

You can find her on Facebook and Twitter, where she loves hanging out with her readers.

Karina is happiest when listening to rock music or riding her motorbike.

More Titles by Karina Kantas

The Outlaw Series
In Times of Violence
Huntress
Lawless Justice
Road Rage

Illusional Reality Duology
Illusional Reality
The Quest
Box set
Audiobook of Illusional Reality
Illusional Reality the Colouring Book
Illusional Reality Journal

Flash and Short Story Collection
Heads & Tales
Undressed
A Flash of Horror

Singles
Stone Cold
Stone Cold Audiobook
Toxic
Broken Chains
In Times of Violence YA Edition

Find all Karina Kantas social links, website and book links here:

http://linktr.ee/karinakantas

www.ingramcontent.com/pod-product-compliance
Lightning Source LLC
Chambersburg PA
CBHW030758190726
48285CB00003B/922